DRIVER'S SEAT

Under the Hood

Book 2

KARLA DOYLE

karla
doyle

Contents

This book was written by a human.
Every sentence came directly from the mind of the author.

This author does not use or support AI-generated content.

Acknowledgments

Thank you to my former bosses and forever friends,
Mark and Gerry, for making it fun to work in an
automotive shop, and teaching me so much about how
vehicles actually work. I love being a full-time author,
but I miss you guys every day.

DRIVER'S SEAT

CAM

After watching the strongest man I've ever known crumble under the weight of a broken heart when my mother died, I made the conscious decision never to fall in love. The best way to do that? Steer clear of women who'll want more than I'm willing to give.

Women like my buddy's little sister, Isabel, who followed me around like a shadow since the day she took her first step, and had our wedding planned and future kids named by the time she was twelve. I was spared the agony of her teenage pining because she moved out of town when her parents divorced.

Now she's back, and according to my buddy, she's in desperate need of a good mechanic. Coincidence? Not likely. I'll service her car as a favor to my friend, but my days of humoring his little sister's crush are over.

Except, Isabel is no longer a little girl and her days of crushing on me are long gone. She's all grown up. A self-assured, interesting, beautiful woman whose only interest in me now is to fix her car. Suddenly, she's in the driver's seat, and it's me who's following her. Crushing on her. Maybe even falling for her…

This book is a standalone story with a happily ever after, and can be read as a solo book. The male main character, Cam, appears as a secondary character in a connected book titled Shifting Gears.

Chapter One

CAM

Fuck me, another one? Cars just keep turning in to the parking lot. This one parks in front of the open bay, despite the large *Do Not Block Bay Doors* sign at eye level on the exterior wall. Some people don't see the signs, others choose to ignore them. Either way, there's a reason for the sign. The moment someone blocks the bay is exactly when we need to pull a vehicle in or out of the shop. Pretty much every damn time.

Normally, I'd holler out at the driver. This time, I don't even turn my head to see who it is. No point hollering for them to move their vehicle. I'm nowhere near finished replacing the alternator on this Cadillac, and I'm sure as hell not bringing another car inside until I finish at least one job. Plus, there's nowhere else for them to park out front. The shop is over capacity.

I've had my bay door open all day, mainly to save those few minutes it takes to raise and lower the thing. Right now, I need every minute I can get. And I can't get enough. Doesn't matter that I've been starting a couple of hours before we open, working through lunch hour, and banging away at jobs long after the doors are locked and the sign says *Closed*. I can't keep up. Each day I'm alone on the job, I fall further behind.

Under the Hood is a two-man shop. Has been since I officially joined the family business, exactly one second after high-school graduation. By the time I completed my apprenticeship, business had nearly doubled, and it continues to grow every year. Dad and I work well together. Same work ethic, same attention to detail and dedication to a job well done. We're run off our feet every day. Sure, we grumble a little from time to time. Shit gets exhausting. But we'd both rather be busy than sitting on our asses in the breakroom.

Customers flocked to the shop back when Dad was a one-man show, just starting out. An honest man who's a quality mechanic doing solid work for a fair price—he always had more demand than he could keep up with. Even with two of us doing the work, there's never a time when our schedule isn't full. It's a rare thing when my sister Shelby can give someone a same-day or next-day appointment without it feeling like she's dropping a half-ton on us. Nobody's getting a rush appointment now. Won't be for a long time.

Hopefully, we won't lose customers permanently. People are understanding in the personal sense, but they need what they need, and if we can't get them in, they'll have no choice but to go elsewhere.

It's been less than a week since my dad broke his hand. Under the Hood is back to being a one-man shop—but with the client base and workload for two full-time mechanics. Dad's going to be off for six weeks, minimum. The doctor might okay him for light duty earlier, but Shelby and I agreed not to let Dad set foot in the shop until he has the final all clear. We both know he'd last all of maybe ten minutes on light duty. Then he'd see something that needs doing, and he'd just do it, setting his recovery back. Maybe injuring himself a different way while compensating. Then we'd be even more fucked.

Until I find a mechanic to help out, I'm on my own. No idea when I'm supposed to review and interview the applicants Shelby keeps adding to the pile of papers on my toolbox. I barely have time to throw back a coffee or take a leak. I can't choose just anybody to fill in, even temporarily. Under the Hood isn't just where I work, it's part of the family.

"Yo, Cam—where are you hiding?"

"In the front end of the silver Caddy." Still elbow-deep in the engine compartment, I crane my neck so my buddy sees my head. "You're right on time. Roll your sleeves up and help me get the belt on this alternator."

Tony coughs up a laugh while picking his way around the disaster covering every visible foot of my bay. "You're going to have to find another helper for that." He runs one clean, probably callus-free hand down his slick, dark-green tie. Always green. The color of money, he says. It's his wardrobe signature. Has been since he got his job selling at BMW. He's good at what he does.

Almost as good as I am at my job. "Unless those pretty-boy shoes have steel toes," I tilt my head downward, "I'm going to need you to stand behind the red safety line."

"What red safety line?" he asks, glancing around on the floor.

Got him. Awesome. "There isn't one, precious."

"Asshole."

"Hey now." I raise an eyebrow when he makes a move like he's going to give me a punch. "You sure about that? Even with my hands currently out of play, you're still only getting one shot off. And the one I'll give you in return isn't just going to hurt, it's going to get grease all over that pristine white shirt." I give him a big grin. "Notice I said pristine and not prissy."

"Dick." He follows the insult with a laugh, then slides his hands into the pockets of black suit pants. "I am a little softer than I used to be, than I'd like to be. We should hit the heavy bags one of these days."

"Sounds good. Not going to happen until my dad's back at work, though. I have less than zero free time until then."

"Yeah, your parking lot is insane. I had to park in front of the bay door."

"That was you?" I pull my hands out of the Cadillac and step around the car so I can check out what he's driving this week. "The M4. Nice."

"You ever want to switch to something new and German, I'll hook you up, man. Say the word."

"Ford."

Another coughed-up laugh bursts from Tony's mouth. "Never going to give them up, huh?"

"Can't. It's in the blood."

Tony nods. Growing up together, he spent nearly as much time at my house as his own, and vice versa. So, he respects the bond I have with my dad that includes a lifelong passion for Mustangs and F-150s—the older the better for both.

"You driving Granger's pride and joy while he's laid up and can't drive stick? I didn't see it parked down the side of the building. Makes sense for you to keep it inside, in your dad's bay, so it doesn't get damaged in that nightmare of cars out front."

Seems the news of my dad's new relationship hasn't spread all over town yet. That's good news, in case things don't work out. Which they won't. Not long-term.

"I've got jobs on his side," I say, jerking my head toward the other side of the shop. The load-bearing wall down the middle obscures most of the view. From Tony's current vantage point, all he can see are my dad's toolboxes. "The Mustang is at his friend's house." The semi-lie curls in my gut. Or maybe that's just fucking hunger, since all I've eaten in the past six hours was a donut for breakfast and the banana Shelby insisted on watching me eat when I wouldn't take a lunch break. "I have to get back to work."

"Sure, I get it." He doesn't, not really.

But that's my problem, not his. "What brings you by, anyway?" I ask as I return to fighting with the alternator belt from hell.

"Yeah, about that."

When that's all he says, I turn my head in his direction and find him wincing. "Spit it out. Since all you drive are demos from the dealership, I know you don't want me to fix a car—thank fuck. You and Vanessa fighting again? Want to grab a beer later, watch the game?"

"Thanks, but no. Vanessa and I are good. Solid and tight, in all the best ways."

"And if you're ever going to want me to sit across from her at a dinner table, then make those your last words on the subject of your sex life."

My buddy grunts a laugh. "When did you flip the maturity switch all the way on?"

A year and a half ago, when my mom died suddenly, and I watched my father, the man who'd always been a rock, crumble under the weight of his grief. "We're thirty, buddy. It was time. So, what do you need that you're chickenshit to ask?"

"To take a quick look at Izzy's car."

"Fuck!" I hiss when I pinch my goddamn finger between the pulley and the belt. Not the Cadillac's fault this time. Distraction gets the blame. I step away from the job, shaking off the sting. "Tell me you're talking about some other Izzy—not your little sister."

"The one and only. But, heads up, don't call her Izzy anymore. She's going by Isabel now. Guess she flipped her maturity switch, too. You should get along great."

"We're not going to get along at all, *Antonio*. First of all, when someone wants a mechanic to 'take a quick look,' it means something went seriously wrong, frequently because they've been ignoring an issue until it's at the breaking point. And as you can see, I don't have time to take anything else on. Not until I find a fill-in tech, and I have no fucking idea when that's going to happen. So, *Izzy*'s going to have to take her problem elsewhere."

"Come on, Cam. You're the best around. The only mechanic—and man—I trust with my baby sister. She can come down after hours if that's better. Just tell her what the car needs, and then if it has to wait until you can squeeze it in, it waits. I just want her to be safe and it really sounds like a piece of shit. Please. I'll owe you, brother."

Asshole, pulling the brother card. He knows family always comes first for me. But I'm still seeing red flags, even if he's not the one holding them. "Was this Izzy's idea? Did she send you down here to ask me?"

Because that would fit. Izzy was infatuated with me since she was old enough to follow me and Tony around. Growing up, the kid was my shadow every time I set foot in their house. Unshakable. Even a locked door didn't keep little Izzy out. Wouldn't surprise me if she became a cop or a private investigator with her lock-picking skills. When she was twelve, she moved away with her mom after their parents divorced, but not before she'd planned our wedding and named our future children. Bad as I felt about their family splitting, I was relieved to see Izzy leave town. Having her pining after me during her teenage years would've been hell.

"Actually," Tony says, lightly tugging at his shirt collar, "she was adamant I *not* ask you. So, I'm going to catch hell about this, but Iz can suck it up for the few minutes she'll have to spend around me."

"Yeah, she'll hate having to be around me again. Right." Winking, I shake my head before going back to the job I need to finish. "Tell her to come by at closing time. I'll get a hoist open and give it five minutes."

"Appreciate it, buddy. So will Izzy."

Appreciation, I can accept. But if Izzy has anything in mind besides car repairs, she's going to be sorely disappointed. I tolerated her over-the-top infatuation when she was a kid. Now that she's an adult, I can be honest with her—I'm never going to see her as anything other than my best friend's little sister.

Chapter Two

ISABEL

The parking lot is full when I get to Cam's shop. Technically, I guess the garage is his dad's business, or possibly the whole family's business, if Cam and Shelby have become partners since I moved away twelve years ago.

Hard to believe it's been that long. Literally half my life ago. I'd just had my twelfth birthday party the month before. I knew my parents argued a lot, that things weren't perfect between them. Being young and naïve, I didn't realize it was serious. Typical kid lack of awareness. I found out the day my mom packed my stuff and loaded me into the car with her. I remember crying my eyes out as we drove away. I didn't understand why we had to leave my dad, my big brother, my school, my friends…and Cam.

The crush I had on my brother's best friend was ridiculous. Since my earliest memories, I had stars in my eyes and butterflies in my belly around Cam. I adored him. Idolized him. I insisted to anyone and everyone who'd listen—Cam included—that I loved him. Little-girl me was sure that one day, when I was older, he'd look at me, have one of those ah-ha moments, then whisk me away for our happily ever after. A big wedding where I'd wear a beautiful white gown. Our two kids—a boy and a girl, naturally. One dog, one cat. A house with a white picket fence.

I had a scrapbook with *all of it*, for crying out loud. I kept that thing for years after moving away, finally parting with it when I turned eighteen. *Eighteen.* If that wasn't the world's longest, most embarrassing crush ever, I dare anyone to show me the person who bested me in the pathetic department.

At least I was infatuated with a nice guy. Despite being good-looking, sporty, popular with friends, and having an endless lineup of drooling girls eager to go out with him, Cam was always, *always*, nice to me. Even when my big brother teased me or flat-out told me to stop bugging them, Cam would be kind. He never laughed or rolled his eyes at me.

Back then, I thought it was because he secretly loved me. Little girls think stupid things.

Shaking off the old memories, along with my irritation at Tony for making me come down here, I park in the only place available in the overcrowded lot—directly in front of the office door. The chime sounds as a man walks out, holding the door for me to scoot inside.

"Thanks," I say, taking my place at the end of a short line.

The three people ahead of me pay their invoices, either making small talk with the young woman on the other side of the counter, or engaging in car-related conversation.

Nobody is a jerk to her. There's no bitching or assholery about the cost of their repairs. Not even from the guy whose bill cost as much as two weeks of my take-home pay.

There's no anger because the customers here know they can trust this shop. Under the Hood has had a great reputation since forever. Everyone in town knows the Smiths are good people. Honest, ethical, caring. Cam's dad set the bar high and from everything I've known and heard over the years, Cam had no problem matching his dad's level of expertise and integrity.

Damn it, even in my head, it sounds like I still have a thing for him. Which I absolutely do not. Respect is not the same as a crush.

"Oh my gosh, Isabel...look at you!" Cam's sister lights up when it's my turn to step up to the counter. "I mean, I've seen pictures of you on Facebook, obviously."

"Good old Facebook." I agree, returning her smile. I'm only two years younger than Shelby, but that gap was like an impassable canyon when we were kids. Being two grades apart in elementary and middle school meant we were never *actual* friends. But our older brothers were the best of friends, and so, our connection continued on, even after I moved away. Shelby and I have been Facebook friends since we set up our accounts—back in the days of getting our parents' permission to add someone.

"You're even more gorgeous in person," she says. "I know you're working as a paralegal, but you could totally be a model."

"Ditto for you. You look—" I catch myself before saying

something that might make her sad. "Way too pretty to be working in an automotive shop."

"And just like my mom. That's what you were going to say, right?" Shelby gives me a warm smile. Either my bitten-back words were written all over my face, or she hears it a lot. Probably both.

"I was going to say that, yes. You were always a mini of your mom, but now that you're an adult, and seeing you in person, the resemblance is even stronger. Your mom was always beautiful, and such a nice person. I'm so sorry for your loss." Eighteen months ago, I sent my condolences in a card. Seems inadequate now that I'm standing in front of Shelby, but what's done is done. "I wish I could've come back for the funeral."

"Don't give that another thought." Shelby reaches across the counter to gently squeeze my hands where I'm twisting them together on the counter. She was always like this, even when we were young. Legitimately good and kind, like every other member of her family. "It's still hard to believe she's gone forever, that I'll never see her again. I know Cam and Dad feel the same way every day. But we lean on each other, keep her memory alive, and work together to go forward, you know?"

Swallowing the lump in my throat, I nod, but in truth, I don't know what she means. My family's dynamic was never like theirs. Tony and I are close, but not like Cam and Shelby. And my parents, well... they're just a totally different breed from Granger and Eline Smith. I know they love me in their own ways, detached or broken as those ways may be.

"So, Tony says your brakes are making noise," Shelby says, releasing my hands and my gaze to return to one of two computers at the service counter.

I open my mouth to answer, but don't get a single word of response out before Cam enters the office through a door behind the counter. Then my mouth goes dry. And words? I have none.

Sweet baby Jesus. My childhood crush is long gone, but my grown-up eyes—and other body parts—are on full alert. Oh sure, I've seen pictures of Cam over the years. Candid shots with friends or family posted by Tony or Shelby. I was well aware that he's gotten better with age. But, like so many things, pictures did not do him justice. Even in his mechanic's uniform, his face shiny and grimy from a hard day's labor, Cam is the hottest man I've ever laid eyes on. It shouldn't even be fair for one man to be this delectable.

"Key?" he says, extending his hand across the counter with the palm up. That's it. No greeting of any variety. No smile. Just a one-word demand.

"Oh, right." I scramble to retrieve my car key from my purse, then remember I stuck it in my back pocket when I came in. By the time I put the key in his waiting hand, my face is on fire. Damn him for throwing me off. Damn *me* for still reacting to him after all these years.

The nod he gives me is so slight, I would've missed it if I'd blinked at the same time. His demeanor changes when he turns his attention to his sister. Still no smile, but his expression softens. There's no bark in his tone when he says, "This test drive will only take a few minutes. You can take off as soon as I pull in. I don't want you to be late for your appointment."

"Are you sure?" Shelby darts a glance my way, as if the question is for me, rather than Cam.

Again, I don't get a chance to answer. Though, this time, it's not because I'm tongue-tied, it's because Cam jumps in first.

"Positive, Shelb. You're on your feet all day and I don't want you to miss a minute of the massage time you booked in advance. Izzy doesn't need you to sit in here and keep her company. She can wait outside while I look at her car after shop hours."

Deserving of the dig as I might be, my hackles go up anyway. I feel like a human hairbrush, I'm so bristly.

Shelby shoots me a grimace after he disappears. "Sorry. He's not usually like that. Since my dad broke his hand and can't work, Cam has been under so much pressure to do everything the two of them do, which is impossible, but he refuses to cancel appointments and disappoint people."

"No apology necessary. I get it, and I don't blame Cam for being irritated. I'm sorry for—" The rest of my apology is cut off by the ear-piercing sound my car makes as Cam drives it into the bay behind the office. The noise is audible even through the closed door separating the two spaces.

"Oh, he's bringing it inside now. He didn't even take it out of the parking lot." An unmistakable look of *that's not a good sign* crosses Shelby's face.

At least I know the money I'm about the hemorrhage will be legit, not a scam. "Don't be late to your massage appointment." I motion for Shelby to get going, then move toward the entrance. "I'll wait out front, like Cam said."

"I'm sure we'll talk soon, and not just about your car," Shelby says, giving me a friendly smile. "Message me if you want to grab a coffee or a drink or dinner sometime."

"I'll do that." Agreeing isn't just a courtesy thing, I think I actually will message her. The few girls I considered friends during childhood don't live in town anymore, and even if they did, I'm not sure I'd reach out to them. People and circumstances change. I know mine have.

With Shelby, it would be a new relationship built on old roots. I could use that kind of fresh start and stability.

A minute later, Shelby hurries out through the open bay, calling a goodbye to Cam. She waves at me, then she disappears down the side of the building, emerging a few seconds later in a small red pickup truck. I get a quick double honk as she drives away.

It's just me and Cam now. Me and the man I was sure I'd marry one day. The man who'd clearly rather be doing anything other than looking at my shitty old car. Or me, for that matter, since he barely acknowledged my presence and literally spoke one word to me. Good thing I wasn't holding on to my silly childhood fantasies.

There are no benches or chairs outside the shop, so I lean against the gray siding near the open bay door, close my eyes, and let the late-day sunshine warm my face. The garage is set back from the road, and it's a not a highly traveled street, even during business hours. The only noise comes from within the shop. Buzzing and clanking from whatever equipment and tools Cam is using, then the loud whine of the big air compressor that drowns out everything, including the sound of my own thoughts.

"Got a couple minutes?"

I shriek and startle at the sound of Cam's deep voice, instinctively lashing out before my eyes are fully open—and making contact. "Sorry," I say when my fist connects with his abdomen, eliciting a groan. "You snuck up on me."

"Not sure that'd hold up in court since you're a customer at my place of business, but you'd be the expert on that."

So, Tony told him I'm a paralegal now. And Cam retained that little nugget of information. Younger me would think that means something about us. Twenty-four-year-old me knows there is no *us*. There never was and never will be. Cam is someone who pays attention to his best friend, that's all.

"I wouldn't have a legal leg to stand on."

His gaze leaves my face to travel downward. "Your legs are a lot longer than the last time I saw you."

Unlike me—and the majority of the world—Cam doesn't have social media accounts. None that I ever found, anyway. He probably hasn't set foot in my dad's house since Tony moved out, and even if he has, there are no recent photos of me on display there. Not that he'd notice if there were.

His attention back on my face, he nods down to where my hands now hang unaggressively at my sides. "You got me pretty good with that jab. Back in the day, you always hung around in your folk's garage while Tony and I hit the heavy bags. Did you start when you got older?" It's casual conversation, probably trying to make up for that blip of being a semi-asshole inside the office a few minutes ago.

But the question pokes a tender spot he doesn't know I have. Tony knows, but I swore him to secrecy. He went against my wishes coming down here to ask Cam to look at my car, but I know my big brother wouldn't betray my confidence about something personal.

"Just some kickboxing classes for a while," I say with a shrug. "I know you're beyond swamped with work, so thanks for putting up with Tony's out-of-line pressure and for taking a look at my car. Give me the bad news, then I'll take the creaky beast and get out of your hair." And it's nice hair. Short and dark, in a style that looks good even after a long day of hot, hard work. I don't have to be infatuated with the man to appreciate his appearance.

"Yeah, about that. You can't drive your car in its current condition. I'll show you what I found so far." Cam motions for me to follow him into the shop.

"What do you mean, *so far?* I drove it all the way from British Columbia, and aside from the scraping noise when I use the brakes, it was fine." I trail after him through the open bay door, bumping into him when he stops in front of me while my focus is trained on my little car, hanging around eye level on a hoist.

"When did you start hearing the brake noise?" He's so close. He didn't put any space between us when I ran into his back. All he did was pivot to face me.

"Um…"

Dark eyebrows descend over his narrowed eyes. "You don't remember, or you don't want to tell me?"

Shit. I've gotten pretty damn good at skirting the truth, but I won't get away with lying about this. Maybe to a mechanic I don't know, but not to Cam. "There was some noise before I left BC, but it just got really bad a couple of days ago."

"You're lucky you made it home, Izzy." The intensity of his stare makes me shiver. Noticeably. And notably, since we're in the middle of a July heatwave, and the temperature inside the shop is even higher than outside, in the blazing sunshine. "Isabel," he says, his voice dropping even deeper with the correction.

The part of me that fell for him all those years ago pops her starry-eyed head up to swoon. I smack the silly little twit down while taking a step back. Doesn't matter how good-looking he is, or if he's being nice to me. Not only is he my brother's best friend, I'm not ready to let any man past the gate.

"Watch your step and your head when you're out here," he says, crooking a finger at me as he moves closer to my car's right rear wheel. "See how this rim is discolored compared to the silver ones?"

"Huh. I hadn't noticed. But I'm never on the passenger side of the car. Why is it like that?"

"Because you kept driving, forcing the wheel to turn while the brakes were locked up, and things overheated." He steps to the front tire and spins it with one hand, then returns to the rear one, puts both gloved hands on the tire and demonstrates its unwillingness to rotate.

"Oh, wow. Yikes. So that's what's causing the noise?"

"That's part of it." Withdrawing a small flashlight from his chest pocket, he beckons me to join him at the front wheel, where he shines the bright, focused beam between the thick spokes of the silver rim. "See there, where the pads sit in the caliper bracket, against the rotor? You literally have no material left. It's metal on metal. They're all like that. It's a miracle they haven't all seized up on you."

"Okay, so, I need new pads on all the wheels," I say, doing my best to sound like I have a single clue what he's talking about. Caliper bracket? Rotor? Does he think regular people know what these things mean? I should've taken auto shop in high school instead of art. But hey, my pointillism skills are kickass. On point, one might say.

The flashlight clicks off. After returning it to his pocket, Cam blows out a long breath while scratching his head, a gesture I doubt has anything to do with being itchy. "Not just pads. The rotors are scored and pitted, so they need replacing too. You're going to need at least the one caliper on the rear, though I wouldn't be surprised if the others will have to be replaced too. I'll service and reuse them if I can, but if the pistons are fucked, they're not going back on the car. And I haven't checked the rest of it over yet."

"God, please don't."

His throaty grunt shouldn't make my nipples stand up, but the girls have never been the best at reading the room. They like what they like, and they like the sound of Cam's voice, even when he's not speaking.

"Should I just drive it to an abandoned field and set it on fire? Wait, pretend you didn't hear me say that. Not that I'm planning to report it as stolen or anything," I say, giving him an exaggerated wink.

The laugh that leaves his mouth this time is the real deal, and it's exactly the way I remember it. "How about I give it a thorough check over and assessment before you commit insurance fraud and arson?"

"I know you don't have time for any of my car crap, Cam. I saw Shelby's Facebook post about your dad being off work for six weeks. I told Tony not to bug you with my problems. Just bring the little shitbox down to the ground and I'll drive it to my dad's—not to a field—and it can sit in the driveway until you're not the only man on the job here."

"You're not bugging me." Again, he scratches his head. This time, while grimacing. "But I can't let you drive this car anywhere. It's not safe. Not even for a short distance."

"So…what? You're going to hold my car hostage?" Prickly heat rises from the pit of my stomach. "Can you legally do that? And before you say yes, you'd better be sure, because I'm damn well going to check when I get to work tomorrow morning, and if you're—"

"Goddamn, Isabel, at least give me the chance to answer before you start throwing the fucking law in my face."

It's not Cam's fault I feel like a trapped animal, but I'm sure as hell not going to explain myself. I can't even force an apology past my lips. The best I can do is cross my arms over my chest and keep quiet.

"I *could* take the plates off your vehicle and call the MTO to report the vehicle as not roadworthy. But I don't want to do that, and I sure as hell don't have time to jump through hoops for the ministry while they investigate. So, as an experienced, licensed mechanic, I'm strongly advising you to leave the car here for repairs, or have it towed somewhere else. And as your friend, I'm asking you to please not put yourself and others in danger by driving this car."

Friend. Not the label younger me had in mind for Cam Smith, but one I'm grateful he's willing to apply now that I'm back in town.

"Okay. I'll leave the car here until you have time for it. And I don't expect you to do it right away—I know there's a long line of customers ahead of me. Plus, I need to get a couple of paychecks in the bank before I can pay for everything the car needs. And if you think it's not worth fixing and I should just scrap it, I will."

"In a field with a gas can and a match?"

"No criminal acts will be committed, I promise," I say, making a cross-my-heart gesture. "And I'm not just saying that to free you from being an accomplice."

He raises his dark eyebrows, a smile pulling his lips into a naturally sensual upward curve.

Just like the old days, my world gets lighter and brighter with his personal sun shining on me.

I jump when the hoist mechanism engages with a loud clunk, followed by a constant hum as the huge apparatus lowers my car to the concrete floor.

"You startle a lot easier now. Nothing spooked you when you were a kid," he says, dark eyes twinkling with amusement. He wouldn't make casual comments like that if he knew why I've become a jumpy adult.

Pushing my nerves and prickly defenses down, I take a silent, calming breath. "I forgot how noisy the equipment is. It's been almost twelve years since the last time—the only time—I was allowed in here."

"I remember that day. Tony came down to tell me he registered for the OMVIC course to get his salesman's license, and you tagged along."

"As always, right?" I say, managing a smile. If my brother never explained why I was clinging to his side that day, I'm not about to. Easier for Cam to assume I insisted on being Tony's sidekick because of my well-known crush. "Thanks for looking at my car. I'll take off so you can close up and go home."

"Yeah, no. I won't be going home for a couple of hours, at least. Too much work to do and not enough hours in the day."

"But…Shelby left. You shouldn't be working on cars with nobody else in the building. What if something happens to *you*, like it did with your dad?" The thought makes my stomach clench.

"I'll be fine. I'm always careful, and that tool breaking for my dad was a freak accident."

"That's exactly my point. Accidents happen even when you're being careful. Does your dad know you're working on cars while nobody else is here? He wouldn't want you doing that."

"You lived on the opposite side of the country the last dozen years, and you've been back in town for a week. I think I know what my dad wants for his business better than you." Cam grunts and shakes his head. "Need anything out of your car before you leave?"

"No."

Without another word, he picks up a tool from the ground, steps to his giant toolbox, grabs something from a drawer, then moves to a pickup truck hanging on another hoist. With an arm raised and the tool in hand, he pauses, looking over at me. "There's going to be noise." Putting me on notice so I'm not startled again. Still a nice guy, even when overworked, stressed to the limit, and annoyed with his best friend's little sister.

I nod and head for the open bay door, but only make it halfway before turning back and walking right up to him. "Your parents always put you and Shelby first," I say when he stops the buzzing and meets my gaze. "And from everything I've heard from Tony over the years, that never changed. So, no, I don't know your dad's business model. But I'd bet that piece of crap," I point to my no-brakes, pitiful little car, "which happens to be the most valuable thing I own, sadly, that your dad cares more about your safety and well-being than this business."

For a long beat, Cam silently drills me with a narrowed stare. But when I walk over to a squatty wheeled stool and plunk myself down, his eyes go wide. "What are you doing?"

"Being your safety crew," I say, pulling out my phone.

"Like hell you are."

"Okay, then I'm keeping you company." My fingers scroll through an endless stream of social media posts, but I don't see any of them. I don't see Cam's face, either, but I can *feel* him glaring at me.

"You're not hanging around for two or three hours tonight while I work on cars."

Now, I look up and meet his hard-ass gaze. "Right. I'll be here *every* night while you work on cars."

Those cartoons where smoke is shooting from the character's ears? That's Cam. His one free hand clenches and flexes at his side, and his jaw is clenched so hard, the animated version of him in my mind would be spitting teeth about now.

I shouldn't find it entertaining. After the shit I've experienced, my flight instincts ought to be in overdrive, but I don't have the urge to get away from him, nor do I feel frozen with fear. Totally irrational, since I haven't seen him for over a decade. He might have a dark side I don't know about. I should be putting *my* safety first, not worrying about his.

My pulse kicks up when he sets the air tool on the ground and closes the distance between us. But I still don't feel unsafe, even when he's hovering over me and I have to tilt my head all the way back to maintain eye contact.

"Isabel." The deep, authoritative way he says my name sends a tingly ripple through me.

"Cam," I say, matching his vibe with a smug smile and an eyebrow wiggle. Can't help it. I always felt safe around Cam, and I still do.

Closing his eyes, he exhales—a long, agonized sound. When he meets my gaze again, his features have relaxed. "You always were an insistent little thing."

"Nice way of saying 'brat.'"

"Nah, you weren't a brat." He winks. "Not as a kid."

Dramatically, I gasp and clutch at my heart, patting around for a couple of seconds before shrugging and dropping my hands. "Nope, not wounded."

"My point proven," he says, shaking his head. "Even though you're not a kid anymore, I could still pick you up and carry you out of here, you know."

The thrill that streaks through me at that prospect is as unwanted as my upcoming car repair bill. I'm not falling for my brother's best friend a second time. "Do what you have to do, Cam. But don't expect that to stop me from doing what I have to do."

He shakes his head, a husky chuckle that makes my nipples hard leaving his smiling mouth. "I'm sure you have better things to do with your free time."

"Not a one." Even now, I can't think of anywhere I'd rather be than in Cam's orbit. What does that say about me?

Before things get weird, I add some awkwardness-decreasing context. "Like you said, I've only been back in town a week. My social calendar hasn't had a chance to fill up yet. Without my car, I'm kind of limited to where I can go, and to be brutally honest, I'm not eager to spend tons of time with my dad. I appreciate that he's letting me stay at his house until I find an apartment, but our relationship has been minimal and strained since my mom left him. I hope things get better between us, but I hate feeling forced into acting like something that we're not. So, if you let me do this for you, you'd be doing me a favor, too. *Another* favor."

Cam doesn't say a word. He just walks to his toolbox, picks up his phone, and initiates a call.

"Are you calling Tony to come get me?" I say, leaping off the stool and storming toward him. "Forget I said anything, Cam. Forget I cared what might happen to you."

Does he listen? No. He dekes sideways when I lunge forward, attempting to grab his phone. The jerk even smiles about it.

"Just hang up." God, I sound pathetic. Which is probably how I've always sounded to him. If he's going to keep treating me like a kid, I might as well act like one, so I stomp my feet, stick out my tongue, and give him the finger before turning on my heel to make a dramatic exit.

"Hey, it's Cam at Under the Hood. Can I get a couple of pizzas delivered? Yeah, we're closed, but I'm still here working. Hang on a sec," he says, then, much louder, "Isabel—you still like pineapple and pepperoni on your pizza?"

It's my turn to be the cartoon character, because I can hear the screeching-to-a-halt sound in my head—that's how abruptly I stop and turn. "What?"

"Pizza. You still eat it?"

"Of course, I do. I'm a brat, not a psycho."

He chuckles, maybe at my retort, maybe at something said on the other end of the call. Either way, amusement is still a good look on him. "How do you like it?"

If he had any idea how many times I imagined him asking me what I like, and not about pizza toppings. "I'm not picky."

"Don't start being accommodating now," he says, driving

my core temperature up several degrees with his sinful smile. "Just tell me what you want."

"Pineapple and spicy sausage. I've upgraded my meat preference." Oh, sure, it could be a casual comment. Innocent. Entirely about processed meat products. And that's what I'd claim in court, even under oath.

But I'd be lying. No matter how much I tell myself I no longer have a crush on Cam, I do. Again, or still, I'm not sure which, not that it matters. Because, to him, I'm never going to be more than his best friend's kid sister.

Knowing nothing's ever going to happen with Cam won't stop me from thinking about *his* spicy sausage. Good thing my vibrator is in better condition than my car, because it's in for a long ride later.

Chapter Three

CAM

I shouldn't have agreed to Isabel's offer—or more accurately, her *demand*—to stick around the shop while I work after hours. Tonight wasn't the first time I've been alone while working on cars, and I'm sure it won't be the last.

When she stormed up to me with her little speech about my parents... I almost gave in then. Because she's not wrong. I know Dad doesn't like all the extra hours I'm putting in since he broke his hand.

He worries that I'm going to burn out and hates not being here to do his share. He built this business from scratch, but I know he'd rather see it fall to the ground than have something happen to me. He still hasn't fully forgiven himself for not being there to protect Mom when she was taken from us—not that he could have prevented the accident, but guilt and logic are hardcore adversaries. I'm not sure he'd survive if something happened to me. Something he'd feel responsible for.

I'd decided to shut shit down and head home once Isabel was gone. Spend some time going through that stack of resumes and make some calls.

Then she shot that plan to hell by parking her cute little ass on the rolling stool and refusing to leave me alone.

In that moment, I realized adult Isabel is exactly the same person as little kid Izzy. Spunky, persistent, wears her heart on her sleeve. I also realized I'll never be able to say no to Isabel, the woman, just like I couldn't say no to the little girl she used to be. I liked that kid. And, even though she's been back in my life for less than an hour, I like the woman she grew into. A little too much, but I'll get a handle on that.

Isabel wanted the fairy tale since she was old enough to talk. She's been gone a long time and I'm sure she outgrew her childhood crush on me, but I doubt her endgame has changed. Little girls with wedding scrapbooks and the names of their future children picked out become women looking for head-over-heels romance with a guy who'll put a ring on it and not hesitate for a second to promise them forever. They want a man like my dad, and a relationship like the one he shared with my mom.

If Isabel had come back to town two years ago, maybe I could've been that man. Not now. Not after seeing how my mother's death affected my dad. After watching the strongest man I've ever known crumble under the weight of a broken heart… Falling in love is off the table for me.

Even if Isabel still has feelings for me, or gets some, I won't go there with her, no matter how gorgeous she is or how much her sassy spirit makes me want to antagonize her and fuck her. Both at the same time would be pretty damn hot. That's going to have to live in my head only. I can't do casual with my best friend's little sister, and I won't do serious with anyone. No love, no loss. No loss, no pain.

"Hey. I don't hear any work happening over there," Isabel says from the chair she brought out from the breakroom after we ate pizza. Her legs are elevated, crossed at the ankles, resting on an open drawer of my toolbox. Total supervisor mode, right down to the tipped-up chin she's giving me.

"Yeah, just zoned out for a minute."

Her feet hit the concrete floor. Within seconds, she's in my space, a serious expression on her face as she checks me over. "It's seven thirty, Cam. Time to call it a day and get some rest." Gentle as her voice is, it's clear she's making a decision, not asking for an opinion.

"Think you're the boss now?" The fact that she's right doesn't mean I can't give her a hard time. Because damn, do I want to give her a *hard time*.

"Self-appointed interim boss of *you*, yes. You have a problem with that, cupcake?"

"Cupcake?" I say on a chuckle, and she gives me a cheeky little smile and nod. Next thing I know, I've got my filthy hands on her lush hips and I'm pinning her to the side of the Dodge I was working on. "You're the only sweet thing here." When her eyes go wide and she sputters instead of sassing me, I wake the hell up and step back. "Shit. I was way out of line, and I'm sorry."

"It's okay. I just——" She snaps her mouth shut, shaking her head. "You're exhausted, and I was teasing, and our signals got mixed-up. That's all it was. A mix-up. No harm done. Let's forget about it."

"I'm not going to forget about it." For more reasons than she'll ever know. "But it won't happen again."

"I know."

"I'll fix this. Make it up to you. Tony just asked me yesterday about getting together to hit the heavy bags. I'll set that up and you can come along. I'll tell him what I did tonight and——"

"No!" A deep blush floods her cheeks as she glances wildly around the shop, looking like a trapped animal desperate to escape. She presses her fingertips to her face, tapping all around while exhaling. "Don't tell Tony," she says, dropping her hands to her sides. "Just...don't. Please."

A nod is all I've got in me. I can't promise to keep my mouth shut after being a complete douchebag to her. Amends need to be made. Taking some punches would be well deserved. "I'm going to shut everything off and get changed. You don't have to wait around. There's a phone list on the desk with the taxi number on it. Call from the office phone and they'll know where to pick you up. Just flip the deadbolt on the office door and you can take off when they get here."

"Sure. Thanks. And thanks for the pizza earlier. It was nice to sit and talk to you for a while."

Every good-mannered word feels like a kick to the balls— which is what I deserve. It's on the tip of my tongue to tell her not to thank me, but I swallow it down. The more I talk about it, the more she has to think about me being a piece of shit.

Without giving her an acknowledgement or goodbye, I head for the stairs that lead to the loft. I take them two at a time, closing the door behind me once I'm inside. There's a shower up here, but I'll wait until I get home, where I can stand under the scalding-hot water until it runs out, even though I know that won't rid me of my shitty feelings.

My shirt is still half buttoned when I hear the monitoring system's robotic voice say "front door open," indicating Isabel left the building. The taxi office is around the block, but it's a big block. There's no way a cab got here that fast. More likely is that she chose to wait outside. Probably couldn't stand to share air with me after I treated her like… like I don't even know what. I've never touched a woman I'm not involved with. And to pin her against the car like I did? I'm surprised she didn't slap me across the face.

Downstairs, I grab the resumes along with my phone and keys. There has to be at least one applicant who can do the job temporarily. Even the small stuff. I don't want Isabel thinking she has to stick to her promise of being my safety crew. Or just as bad, maybe worse, if she *doesn't* show up to keep her promise. I just need to hire someone tomorrow. Eliminate both options and all the problems.

I shut off the compressor and torch, check all the doors, then hit the lights, set the alarm, and head outside. It's not fully dark yet, but twilight hangs low and heavy, painting the horizon in swaths of orange, pink, and blue.

Isabel is nowhere to be seen. She must've called from her phone, out here in the parking lot, and got a driver immediately. Good. Waiting with her would've been awkward. Earlier, I had planned to offer her a ride. Be a nice guy. I sure fucked that up.

After checking all the car doors in the lot to make sure they're locked, I hop into my truck, parked beside the building. The drive to my house takes the same amount of time no matter which direction I turn, but I always make a right. Tonight, I take a left, and I see the reason for my gut feeling comes into view before I reach the stoplights.

Isabel, walking. She's on the opposite side of the street, but there's no traffic, so I slow to a crawl and roll my window down.

"Couldn't get a taxi?" I call across the open lane.

"Didn't try."

"Are you taking a bus?"

"No," she says, shaking her head. "I'm going to walk."

"It'll take you an hour to get to your dad's place. And it'll be fully dark soon. I know you've been a city girl for the past twelve years, but I don't like the idea of you walking alone at night. If you don't want to ride with me, let me call a cab, or your brother."

She stops on the sidewalk, forcing me to do the same in my lane. "You didn't offer me a ride."

"I didn't think you'd want one after what I did." Behind me, an approaching driver honks their horn. I put on my four-ways and stick my arm out the driver's window, motioning them to go around.

"Ask me," Isabel says, after the car passes.

One hand on top of the steering wheel, I crane my upper body so I'm kind of sticking out the open window. "Can I give you a ride? If you're not comfortable with me, and won't let me call someone else to pick you up, then I'll match your speed and drive beside you to make sure you get home safely."

"So, you're *my* safety crew now?" Even from across the lane, the playfulness in her tone is clear. As is the smile on her face.

I can't resist sending the same back. "The self-appointed boss."

Her laughter floats on the clear night air, straight into my head, where I'm giving the sound permission to live rent free. Then she jogs across the street and hops up into the passenger side of my two-door F-150. "Thank you for the ride. And before you apologize again about what happened in the shop, don't. You read the room correctly—I was flirting a bit. I guess I thought it was safe to flirt with you because you're my brother's best friend, and you'd never be interested in me that way. Under other circumstances, I would have reacted differently to having a good-looking man press me up against the door of a car. It was just unexpected from you."

"It was unexpected *for* me, too. I don't do hands-on without permission. I don't know what possessed me to do that with you, of all people. You were practically my little sister when you were a kid."

"But I'm not a kid anymore."

"No, you're definitely not." It takes all my willpower to keep my attention on her face. Even sitting beside me in the semi-dark, it's still plenty clear she's all woman now.

"So…we're good?" She raises her eyebrows at me while buckling in. "No more apologies, no awkwardness. We acknowledge that I was just being a flirty girl, and because you're only human, you couldn't resist me, but it was a momentary lapse in judgement on both our parts."

I chuckle under my breath while resuming driving. "Sounds about right." Especially the part about being unable to resist her. My reaction to her was instinctual. Automatic. Not like me at all.

"I'm glad. I'd hate for a single stupid moment to come between us now that we're old enough to be friends."

Friends. That word would normally be like an ice bath. The ultimate dick shrinker. It's having zero effect on me right now. Being in the truck cab with Isabel, surrounded by the light scent of her perfume, my mind replaying how soft she felt against me for those few seconds in the shop… Shrinkage is definitely not my issue.

"Single stupid moment already forgotten," I lie, keeping my eyes on the road. "How about you?"

"Same. I don't even know what moment you're talking about."

When I glance over, she looks relaxed and unfazed. The opposite of my internal short-circuiting. She must've been telling the truth about just being the flirty type and thinking I was in the safe zone. I should be relieved.

"Is this the same truck you had before I moved?" she asks, running her hands over the upholstery.

"It is. Ninth gen F-150. The last year they made this style."

"They all look the same to me."

I shoot her the side-eye. "They're not all the same."

"It's cute how you geek out about car stuff. Still, you never wanted something different?"

"Why would I?"

"Because you could have whatever truck you want. Don't you ever just want to change vehicles because you're bored with having the same one forever? Out with the old, in with the new. That's what people do."

"I don't want something new; I want this truck. I take care of it, I know everything about it, and it never lets me down. It's comfortable and reliable and beautiful, and I still enjoy the ride every time I get in. I'm not interested in other trucks."

"Wow, Cam. That's so romantic. I hope you and your truck will have a long and happy life together."

"Good one, little brat."

"Not so little," she says, settling in against the backrest. "Puberty gave me more than the standard allotment of curves. Then the freshman fifteen got me during college, and invited fifteen more hip-hugging friends, all of which stayed, as I'm sure you noticed during the moment that never happened."

The urge to tell her she's the perfect size is on the tip of my tongue. If she were any woman other than Isabel Burns, I'd look over and let her know how much I loved the way her full hips felt in my hands. That her softness makes me so fucking hard. That I've taken every possible opportunity to check out her juicy round ass and my palms are itching to squeeze it.

But I won't tell her all that because she's not any other woman. Not someone I can have a quick, hot fling with. She's my best friend's little sister. Off-limits to me *and* not interested in me. Double whammy. So, I clench my jaw and say nothing. Do nothing. Just drive my *friend* home.

WHAT WOULD'VE BEEN an hour-long walk is a ten-minute drive. I haven't been to the Burns' place since Tony moved out. The house Isabel spent the first twelve years of her life in is looking pretty rough, even in the dim light of near dark.

Tony doesn't say much about his parents—never did, even back when the split happened—but it's no secret around town that his dad is an alcoholic with a history of spending more on booze than he can afford. Somehow, Edward Burns managed to hang on to the house. But it couldn't have been a great homecoming for Isabel, coming back to find it so rundown.

Isabel is out of my truck the moment I stop in the driveway. "I'll see you tomorrow, shortly after five o'clock." Standing on the asphalt with one hand holding the truck door open, she points a finger at me. "And don't start with me about not needing a babysitter. The only way you're getting rid of me is if you find a replacement."

"Pretty sure you're the only person who wants the job." And definitely the only person I want to have it. "Have a good night."

She closes the door, waves, then moves toward the side door of the house, waving again before unlocking it and disappearing inside.

Simultaneously relieved and disappointed to watch a woman walk away. First time for that sensation. Fuck.

Chapter Four

CAM

"Want me to stay for the interviews?" Shelby asks after locking the customer door at closing time.

"Nah, I can handle it. You've listened to enough people today."

My sister took over running the office end of things when our mom died. She'd helped out before then, but there's a big difference between part-time assistant to your mother, and the shitload of duties and responsibilities that come with being the solitary office manager. Especially in a small shop like ours.

Shelby has come a long way in eighteen months. Knows a hell of a lot more about cars and how they work, can estimate almost any repair job on her own, talks with parts suppliers with confidence, juggles the constantly ringing double phone lines like a magician. But when a customer goes asshole on her... she hasn't learned to navigate that shit yet. Fortunately, it doesn't happen often.

It's usually Dad who has her back when it does. Because his bays are directly behind the office, and even when he's busting his ass on cars, he still has one eye on the front. Even though Shelby is twenty-six, she's still Daddy's little girl, and he swoops in to the rescue. Plus, it's his business, and customers like talking to "the owner." Someone who might not accept Shelby's word on their car troubles will almost always respect my dad's.

Today was one of those days when Dad's presence was sorely missed. By the time Shelby came out to my bay on the opposite side of the shop, she was in tears because some idiot up front was giving her shit about the quote for his repairs. Knowing how fucking slammed with work I am, she tried to field all the questions and snarly comments on her own, but she still doesn't have adequate knowledge. The asshole on the other side of the desk smelled blood and went in for the kill.

My dad has a calmness about him that can defuse just about any conflict. I'm like him in many ways, but that's not one of them. I wasn't completely unprofessional to the guy who insulted my sister. But I didn't take the time to hear him out or answer his questions. I just walked into the office, ripped up his quote, and told him to find another shop.

Bad for business? Possibly. Good for my sister's mental health? Fucking right, it was.

"If you're sure..." Shelby glances over at me while inputting all the daily numbers in the spreadsheets she inherited from our mom.

"Positive, Shelb. It's only two people, because that stack of

42

applicants was basically a pile of shit, and I'm talking to them together to save time."

She wrinkles her nose at me the way she's done since we were kids. "Is that how technicians are usually interviewed?"

"No idea. I've never had an interview."

"I know that, *obviously*. I just thought you might've called Tim or Kenny, or one of the other many friendly industry people you're acquainted with, for some advice." She rolls her eyes when I look at her as if she just suggested I drink a big glass of sour milk. "You're a great mechanic, Cam. Everybody in town knows that. Nobody would think less of you because you ask for some hiring tips before you take your first crack at it."

"I don't need help figuring out who'll be a good tech. I'll know."

"God, you're stubborn." Shelby shakes her head while grabbing her purse from the adjacent breakroom. "Am I right, Isabel, or am I right?"

Pretty sure my head has never snapped around as fast it does when I follow the line of Shelby's gaze.

"One hundred percent," Isabel says, approaching the counter. She must have come into the shop through the open bay, then into the vestibule through the parts delivery door, neither of which would make the monitoring system ping. She folds her arms on top of the counter as if being here is an everyday thing. Like she's been here all along. Like she's one of us.

I could get used to that. Hell, I'm already used to it.

Yesterday afternoon, I was pissed off that I let Tony guilt me into looking at Isabel's car. I didn't want to have to face the girl who'd followed me around like a lovesick puppy. Flip the calendar one day and it's a whole other story. I've been watching the damn clock all day, waiting for her to get here, hoping she didn't decide not to bother. I can't take my fucking eyes off of her. Who's the puppy now?

"What's he being stubborn about today?" Isabel's full pink lips form a smile that's directed at me.

"Won't ask for help," Shelby says, cutting around the counter.

"Shocking."

Shelby laughs, pausing to pat Isabel's shoulder. "You're back one day and you already get him."

"Yeah, but I've heard he's not hard to get."

"Ouch, burn." Shelby leans over the counter and presses a finger on me, making a sizzling noise. Taking a page out of Isabel's book. Having lighthearted fun for the first time in longer than I can remember. "Actually, Cam has settled down a lot the past couple years. Though, that might be because he's run through all the single ladies in town and is out of options. Ooh, but now you're here." My sister's gaze darts between Isabel and I. "And there's definitely chemistry..." she singsongs.

"Friendship chemistry, that's all." One of Isabel's perfect, dark eyebrows rises. "Besides, I found out last night that Cam already has a true love." She leans in as if she's going to tell Shelby a secret, but her gaze is still tethered to mine as she says in a full-volume mock-whisper, "He's in a committed, long-term relationship with his truck."

Shelby erupts in a fit of giggles. "Oh, I knew that already. But did you know he's polyamorous?"

"What the fuck is polyamorous?" I cut in.

The women ignore my question, continuing to talk about me as if I'm not sitting right in front of them.

"And he gave me this heartfelt speech about how he'd never want any other truck." Hand on her chest, Isabel looks me up and down—what she can see of me, anyway. "Not going to lie, I was moved. Now, I feel so dirty for believing him."

I shake my head and roll my eyes. It's for show, just like Isabel's act. The way her playful teasing makes me feel is real, though. Good in a way I've never experienced.

Shelby's enjoying the Isabel effect, too. She's been so serious since our mom passed. She deserves this moment of fun and camaraderie.

"Oh, his other one isn't a truck. Well, not technically," Shelby says. "Pretty sure that's why he thinks it's okay to enjoy them both. Not only that, they're…*related*."

"No," Isabel hisses.

"Yup." Shelby nods. "Same parent company."

"I'm scandalized." Isabel places the back of one hand on her forehead, using the other to fan herself. "I never thought Cam would be the kind of man to *Ford around*."

Another round of rowdy yet feminine giggles fill the office. The place feels alive again.

"All right, comedy hour's over, wiseasses," I say, pointing at the door when I see two cars pull into the parking lot. "My interviewees are here. With any luck, one of them will start tomorrow."

"Fingers crossed!" Shelby gives the gesture to go with her words, then waves at Isabel and leaves through the customer door, leaving it unlocked.

Isabel joins me behind the counter, making herself at home on Shelby's preferred stool. "Hiring someone would mean you'd stop working after the shop is closed?"

"Ideally, yeah. Knowing you'll be hanging out here every night lit a fire under my ass to get someone in here, ASAP."

"I see." She hops off the seat as the monitoring system announces the front door opening with the arrival of the potential hires. "I'll wait outside while you do your interviews. Good luck."

It's a hot, sticky, July afternoon, and there's no AC in here, yet when Isabel walks past me, I swear there's an ice-cold breeze.

ISABEL

There's no shade and nowhere to sit in front of the shop. I was overheated when I got here—biking in the blazing sunshine will do that—but the level of heat churning inside me now makes my previous body temperature feel like I went for a polar-bear dip. Every second I think about Cam pushes me closer to erupting in flames.

Not sexy flames, like last night, when he grabbed my hips and pressed me against the car he was working on. Sweet baby Jesus. Yes, *I* froze up, but the moment itself was hot.

But nothing happened, and *this* hot moment is the complete opposite—though not unrelated, which makes me even madder. Which then makes me even hotter. I'm a mess. A hot, miserable, sexually frustrated, emotionally tangled mess.

I should just leave. That's what he wants. He told me so last night, point blank. But did I listen? Of course not. Do I ever do the sensible thing? Rarely. If that was my MO, I wouldn't have peeled out of my previous life like *my* ass was on fire.

Forcing myself on Cam after hours was rooted in sensibility, though. It isn't safe for him to work alone. I saw firsthand how tired he was. Accidents can happen anytime, but working while exhausted certainly increases the likelihood.

I care about him, even after being gone for twelve years. Also, no matter what decision I made about not having a crush on him anymore, the stupid feelings came rushing back the minute I saw him. My heart is all "fuck your *decisions*, lady, I want what I want" and it still wants Cam.

Too bad I'm not ready to want Cam, and he clearly doesn't want me, despite our brief sexy-hot moment.

"That was fucking weird."

At the sound of a male voice that doesn't belong to Cam, I tuck myself around the corner of the building, out of sight, then angle to get a sliver of a peek at the voice's owner. Both guys Cam is supposed to be interviewing are in the parking lot already.

"I've never been to an interview where I'm not the only candidate in the room. But whatever. It was the lack of questions that's fucked up," the same voice says as the guys walk to their respective vehicles. "And then to tell us both no thanks? Based on what, buddy? Our haircuts?"

Guy number two snorts. "Maybe he didn't know what to ask, what with it being a family business and all. He got his job the easy way."

"Good point," guy number one agrees.

Not that long ago, I'd have gotten in their faces and given them the hell they deserve for shit-talking about Cam. Now, all I can do is stand there and silently seethe. Those pricks have no idea how hard Cam works. He didn't get his position easily, because his dad handed it to him. He earned it.

"There you are," Cam says when I step out from my hiding place after their cars pull away. "I thought maybe you left."

"I considered it." I tip my chin up. Just because I feel defensive about him doesn't give Cam a pass for what he said to me in the office. "But it's unsafe for you to be banging away on cars with nobody else around, so, sorry about your shitty luck, but you're stuck with me until you replace me. Also, I'm still too damn hot from the trip over here to get back on my bike and ride across town." I hook a finger in the direction of the street. "I take it the interviews didn't go well. Not surprising, they were obviously jerks."

Cam's dark eyebrows draw together, creating furrows on his forehead. "How do you know they were jerks? Did they say something to you? *Do* something?" At his sides, his hands curl into fists. "Is that why you were down the side of the building?"

I can be pissed off at Cam and still appreciate his protectiveness toward me. It's one of the things I used to love about him. Wherever Cam was, was the safest place in the world. It still might be. "They didn't even know I was out here. I overheard them talking about how you barely asked them any questions before turning them down."

"I didn't have to ask a lot to know neither of them was right for the job."

"Then there's no point wasting more time on them. You'll know the right person when you find them."

"Yeah," he says, his eyes traveling over my face. "I think I will."

Little butterflies take wing in my belly. Foolish, infatuated butterflies that would like his words and gaze to mean more than they do.

"Did you really ride your bicycle over here? And to work this morning?" He rubs his fingers back and forth over his head when I nod. "Couldn't get a taxi?"

"Didn't try. Cabs aren't cheap, and I'm saving my pennies to pay for that hot mess," I say, pointing at my car, where Cam parked it until he has time to fix it—which could be weeks away. "And first and last on an apartment, when I find one. Plus, there's nothing wrong with biking."

"Except sweating your ass off and potentially getting struck by a motorized vehicle."

"I rode on the sidewalk."

"Still not safe." A pained, heaving sigh leaves his handsome face. "Did you at least wear a helmet?"

"I would have if I had one. I get half marks for that, right?" I ask in my *look how cute I'm being* voice, which totally misses the mark, based on his scowl.

"You get zero marks, Iz. For someone who's so concerned about my safety, you're pretty lax with your own."

"Well, for someone who can't wait to be rid of me, you sure seem to care if I'm okay."

"Of course I care," he says. No denial about wanting to be rid of me. At least he's not a liar.

"I know you care." I sigh. "I'm your best friend's little sister."

"That's part of the reason. Not all of it. I've always liked you for you. Even when you were a kid. And now that you're not a kid…"

We're outside, yet it feels like all the air has been sucked out from between us. Like we're vacuum-sealed in a bubble that the wrong word or action could burst.

But I can't say nothing. I have to know. "And now that I'm not a kid…what, Cam?"

"You're even more likeable. Likeable in ways I wasn't prepared for, and can't commit to."

"Because your heart belongs to your immaculate, ninth-gen F-150 and whatever mysterious Ford sibling you've got stashed away somewhere, I know." Humor is the saver of all things. My go-to diversion technique to prevent the big, bad serious thing, whatever that thing might be.

It doesn't always work. Right now, with Cam, it has the desired effect, because a smile replaces his *everything is doomed, run for your life!* expression.

"On the subject of my other Ford," he says, motioning for me to follow him. "How do you feel about closing up shop for the day, tossing your bike in the back of my truck, and going for a drive with me?"

"Don't you have at least three more hours of work to do before you start all over again tomorrow at the butt crack of dawn?" I trail him into the garage, scooting out the way as he uses a heavy chain mechanism to manually lower the bay door, then secures it with a thick, flat deadbolt.

"*Before* the butt crack, Isabel."

"Oh shit. I just realized that I should be here for those hours, too. God, babysitting you is a lot of work."

"Having second thoughts about volunteering?"

I shrug. "Maybe one or two."

"Pretty low, considering. But you get a break tonight. Just this once, work is going to take a backseat."

"Get back there, endless list of jobs." I make a whipping gesture, complete with perfect sound effects. "Cam's in the driver's seat tonight." I may never be more to him than his best friend's little sister, a semi-annoying goofball friend, but being that, and making him laugh... way better than hanging on to old fantasies from a wedding scrapbook.

Chapter Five

CAM

Not flirting with Isabel might be as impossible as not breathing. I know I'm sending her mixed signals. Hell, I'm sending myself mixed signals.

I might think she's doing the same if she hadn't looked me in the eye last night and told me she was flirting but didn't mean anything by it because I'm her brother's best friend. That's how she sees me now, as a friend. A guy she can safely flirt or joke around with, knowing nothing's going to come of it. Nothing is at stake. I'm no longer the man in her happily ever after scrapbook.

Except…if I'm her buddy, and she's not interested in more, why'd she get so pissed off about me working to end to her after-hours hangouts? A beautiful, sexy, funny woman shouldn't be spending her off-hours in an automotive shop. There have to be a dozen other things she could be doing. If it's the lack of transportation that's stopping her, I have the fix.

"Oh wow, it's like time stood still while I was gone. This is exactly how I remember it looking," she says as I turn off the busy, north-south street onto a narrow one that winds through what everyone to as *old heights*, even though the neighborhood isn't that old or high. "How long have you lived in this part of town?"

"Five years. I bought an estate sale property that'd been on the market for a long time. It's a tiny two bedroom and needs a lot of updating. But the detached garage is solid, heated, and big enough that I had room to install the old drive-on rack from the shop when we replaced it, and I can still park two vehicles comfortably."

"Ah…there it is. The true selling point." The smile on her face when I glance over nearly makes me jump the curb. "Why do you need old shop equipment in your home garage?"

"Because passion projects aren't short term."

Her soft sigh floats on the warm air coming through my truck's open windows. "A lot of women dream of finding a man who will feel and talk about *them* the way you do about your vehicles."

"And you're one of them." I laugh when she reaches across to punch my arm. "Don't tell me you're denying it. I've seen the scrapbook."

She covers her face with her hands. "You remember that thing?"

"How could I forget? You showed it to me every chance you got."

"What a maniac I was." She shakes her head, the breeze from the open window making the ends of her shiny auburn hair dance. "But you were always really nice to me. Which only encouraged me, you realize," she says, following it with one of those exaggerated evil laughs, just like her younger self used to make.

"Not going to lie, when you hit twelve years old and were still adding stuff to the scrapbook, I started to get seriously concerned." I grin at her while making the last turn toward my house. "Like, restraining order concerned."

"You're not wrong, I was a little obsessed." She spreads her arms as wide as possible in the two-seater cab of my truck. "But I'm over it, I promise. Your days as my scrapbook husband and the father of my magazine cutout children are long gone."

And now we're friends. Talk about being downgraded.

"This is it." I pull into the single-wide driveway and park back a ways from the garage. "Nothing like the big, fancy house pics in your scrapbook."

"Those were silly childhood ideas about what a happy life would look like," she says, her gaze moving over the property, taking it in. "This is cute and down to earth. An actual home. Much better than the scrapbook."

"You might want to reserve judgment until after you've seen the wallpapered bathroom with its pink toilet, sink, and tub."

"You're going to give me the full tour?" Her eyes go wide with excitement. The same way they did when Tony and I would let her go places with us. "I thought you were just going to show me your sidepiece vehicle."

I shake my head while getting out of the truck. If I'd

known how awesome she'd be as an adult, would I have stayed in touch with her after she left?

There's a grunted *oof* as she collides with my back when I stop dead in my tracks. The what the fuck expression on her face morphs into confusion when she looks up at me. "Are you okay? You look stressed-out all of a sudden. Thinking about how much work you blew off tonight? Because we can go back to the shop if you need to."

Agreeing would be an easy out. The best way to keep things casual and safely in the friend zone. "I'm sorry I never answered your letters or cards. Ignoring them was a dick move."

"Oh." It comes out so softly, it wouldn't be audible if she wasn't practically tits to chest with me. "I haven't thought about all that for a long time."

"Me either. I filed it away under 'things that'll never matter,' but I was wrong to think that. Your feelings mattered."

"You were eighteen when I moved out west, Cam. Way too young to be responsible for making a sad, homesick little girl who meant nothing to you feel better."

I could tell her she meant something to me, but the truth is, I was relieved when she moved across the country with her mom. All I can do is be there for her now, which is why we're here. "How about I make it up to you?"

"With a fat discount on my car repairs?" she asks, wiggling her eyebrows. "Just kidding. I would never ask for or expect a discount."

"I already told Shelby to give you the friends and family rate when she does your invoice." Putting my hand on her lower back to direct her toward the garage sends a streak of awareness through me. "I have something else in mind for you right now."

"I think I've seen this porno before."

A deep chuckle rolls out of me, natural as breathing. "I've laughed more in the past twenty-four hours than I have in…well, eighteen months."

"You've been through a lot in that year and a half," she says, a gentle smile on her lips when she looks up at me while we walk. "I'm glad I can provide some comic relief. And since we're on the subjects of sad times and regrets, I'm so very sorry for your loss. I wish I'd been able to come back for the funeral."

"I'm glad you didn't. I was a mess. The whole family was. If you'd walked right up to me, I wouldn't have seen you." I unlock the garage's man door, meeting her eyes as I slip the keys into my pocket. "And that would've been another loss."

Her lips open and close, wordless. Then she blinks and the sass returns to every part of her face. "Geez, Cam. It's almost like you *want* me to start a new scrapbook."

Maybe I do. Maybe I fucking do. "Come on, smartass." The motion-activated lights come on as soon as we step inside. I nod toward the mostly finished Bronco. "Still needs a paint job, but there she is."

"She?" Isabel circles the vehicle, snorting after leaning inside through the open driver's side window. "It's so old-fashioned. Is *she* a senior citizen?"

"She's a classic." The urge to smack Isabel's ass as I walk

past almost wins. Not something opposite-sex *friends* do. "Hop in."

Uncharacteristically, she follows my instructions. "It *is* pretty cool," she says, running her hands over the buttons and dials of the refinished, original equipment dashboard. "Does it run?"

"Better than the day it rolled off the lot, back in 1990."

"Holy shit, it's practically a relic."

"She's gotten better with age." Not unlike the woman in the driver's seat.

"Okay, seriously. What's with the 'she' bit?"

"You really want to know?" I raise an eyebrow, as if I'm daring her to say yes.

"Wait, let me guess." Her eyelids flutter to half-closed, then her tongue glides along her lips, leaving them glistening. "When you slide inside her, enjoying the sensation of her silky soft interior against your skin, then you turn her on and her engine purrs, reminding you of the sound a woman makes when you're going full throttle on her, her..." Isabel's eyes pop open to their full, bright size. "Shit, I can't think of a good car part to use as a euphemism for clit. Got any suggestions?"

"Not currently," I say, my voice coming out hoarse.

"So? Did I guess right? It has something to do with sex, the reason you call it 'she.'" The throaty tone from before is gone. Just another thing she did for effect, to get a reaction.

And it worked. My body's reacting, all right. If I have to get out of my seat anytime soon, she'll see exactly how her borderline dirty talking affected me. "You weren't even close." I pop open the glove box and retrieve a folded piece of paper. "Original ownership," I say, handing her the form. Electricity races up my arm when our fingers touch, and I barely contain my needy groan.

"Violet Macauley." Isabel's gaze snaps to mine. "Awww, Cam, you call the Bronco a 'she' because the original owner was a woman?" She reaches over and pinches my cheek the way a grandmother would. "You big softie, you."

Instinct makes me catch her wrist before she can pull her hand away.

Her breath catches, her eyes going wide as I draw the mount of her palm to my mouth and graze my lips across her soft skin. "Cam… what are you doing?"

"I don't know. Something I shouldn't? You tell me, Iz."

"You…probably shouldn't," she whispers.

"Right." I nod, releasing my hold. "Friends."

"It's not that I don't find you attractive. I do."

"But I told you I can't commit, and you're not a friends-with-benefits girl."

"I'm not an anything girl right now. There's a shitty ex-boyfriend to blame for that. More than one, actually." Rolling to her back, against the driver's seat, she grabs the steering wheel and stares out through the windshield. "You're probably sitting over there thinking, typical woman, blaming the guy."

"Actually, I was thinking he must be a fucking idiot, letting you get away." My answer doesn't get the response I expected. It doesn't get any response at all. At least my hard-on is gone, so I can circle back to something good, the reason I brought her here. "Buckle up while I open the garage door. You can ask me anything you might need to know about the Bronco while we take your loaner for a spin."

I'm halfway to the door when she leans out the driver's window and calls, "What do you mean, *my loaner?*"

The hum of the garage door opener gives me an excuse not to answer. Out in the driveway, I hop in my truck and pull it into the empty spot next to the Bronco.

"Yoo-hoo, over here…" Isabel sticks her arm out her window, waving it around as if she's trying to flag down a waiter.

To look at her is to see a beautiful woman. To spend five minutes with her is to know she's adorable. Irresistible. I'm starting to think spending a lifetime with her might be the stuff scrapbooks are made of.

Back in the passenger seat, I clip the spare garage door remote to the sun visor, then fasten my seatbelt. "Start her up and take her out."

Big brown eyes blink at me. "You seriously want *me* to drive this?"

"That is what I said."

"You also said 'loaner,' then failed to answer me when I asked for clarification."

"It's a pretty straightforward term. Loaner—something borrowed during a repair period. I'm repairing your car and giving you the Bronco as a loaner."

"After listening to you moon about your vehicles, there's no way in hell I would borrow one of them. What if I damage it?"

"I know a good shop. Kind of hard to get an appointment, but I'm confident the mechanic there would squeeze you in. He thinks you're cute and you make him laugh."

"Cam."

Yeah, it's happening. I'm becoming addicted to the sound of my name in her voice. No matter what tone she uses.

"This gesture, your offer, is the sweetest, most generous thing ever. But I can't accept. It's too much. I mean, you barely know me."

"I've known you since the day you were born. Yeah, you moved away for a while. That doesn't make us strangers. It just means we have some catching up to do." When the only response I get is the torture of watching her chew on her full bottom lip, I take a breath and play another angle. One that's less *sweet.* "Borrow the truck instead, if you prefer. But you either borrow one of my vehicles, or I rearrange my schedule to drive you everywhere you need to go. At all hours. And you know how fucked my schedule is, so you'd be inconveniencing the shit out of me, but I'll do it."

"You're a bully," she says, reaching for key I always leave on the dashboard. "And a good friend."

There's that word again. The more she says it, the less I like the sound of it.

"Where should I go for my driving test?" She gives me a saucy smile while starting the engine. "Since I know that's what this is."

"How about Cabella's?"

"The Italian restaurant out on Highway 2?"

"Yeah. Nothing's changed since you left. They still make the best meatballs."

She wiggles her eyebrows. "You just want to see how many balls I can fit in my mouth, admit it."

"You got me," I say, shaking my head. Though, now that she suggested it, I have a clear mental picture of her fitting both my balls in her mouth. Good thing we have a fifteen-minute drive ahead of us. Hopefully, it's enough time for *this* hard-on to go down.

"Then it's a date. A friend date. But you can still buy. This time, because I'm basically broke. We can go out again after I've paid my car repair bill and I'm back on my feet financially, and I'll pay then."

My nod is a lie. There's no way I'll wait that long to take her out again. And I'm always going to pay. I'm always going to take care of her needs—in as many ways as she lets me.

Chapter Six

ISABEL

When I pull into Under the Hood's parking lot at six o'clock on Friday evening, both bay doors are shut and the sign in the office window is turned to *Closed*. Shelby's small truck is gone and Cam's is parked down the side of the building. First one in, last one out. He says that's always been his dad's thing. Now it's his turn.

The lot is still full of customers' cars, something I've learned is a stressor for Cam, another trait he inherited from his dad. They prefer to get vehicles in and out, same day if possible. Having this many vehicles lingering overnight, day after day after day… it's why Cam is putting in all the extra time after regular business hours. And if he's here, I'll be here to make sure he's not alone, in case of an emergency. That's what I told him on Tuesday, and I've kept my word. Wednesday, though…

Wednesday could've been plucked from the pages of my *Cam and Izzy Forever* scrapbook. That moment in the garage

at his house where he sort-of kissed the base of my hand...
It was as unexpected as him loaning me one of his vehicles.
His gentle, chaste yet sensual touch set off fireworks inside
me. My brain was quick to snuff them out, but for those
few seconds, I thought... maybe.

Then I maybe'd myself throughout our not-a-date dinner
date. What woman wouldn't love being the center of
Cam's attention in a cozy booth at a delicious restaurant?
If he'd tried to kiss me goodnight, I might have let him.
Solid maybe. But he didn't—because I friend-zoned him.
That part wouldn't have been in the old scrapbook. Little
girl me would never put Cam in the friend zone. Back
then, I knew, without a doubt, what I wanted. I could go
for some of that certainty now.

Last night, we sat together in the shop's breakroom and ate
the sandwiches I brought. A chef, I am not. Cam didn't
mind the simple supper. And I sure didn't mind watching
him eat. The man makes chewing sexy. Who am I kidding?
He makes everything sexy. After our quick meal, he went
back to his bay, banging away at jobs until nearly eight
o'clock, only stopping when I caught him rinsing out a
deep gash in his index finger, and forced him to call it
a day.

I'm torn between wanting him to hire a tech because he
needs the help, and selfishly hoping I get to keep having
this time with him five days a week until his dad returns to
work.

But tonight—tonight, I wish I didn't have to go inside.
Because I'm late, and that's going to lead to questions I
don't want to answer. I want to be the person who makes
Cam laugh and smile. He's the best part of moving back
here, and I'd rather not tell him about the worst.

After one more check of my face in the rearview mirror, I lock the Bronco and head in through the customer door, turning the deadbolt behind me. Paper takeout bags on the breakroom table catch my eye as I pass. Two of them, both still folded and stapled across the top. He had dinner delivered. And waited for me to eat it.

"Hey," he calls when he spots me coming through the office door. "I guessed you had to work late, so I ordered some Kung Pao, General Tso, and pineapple chicken balls. I remember those used to be your favorite."

This is where I should make some sort of *balls* joke, or tease him with a double entendre. But nothing comes to me. "Okay, thanks. Whenever you want to take a break."

The furrows that form on his forehead are visible from across the bay. Then his tools are on the ground and he's cutting a path straight for me. "What's wrong?"

"I didn't crack up the Bronco."

"I wouldn't give a shit if you did, as long as you're okay."

"I'm fine."

"No, you're not," he says, stepping closer. Close enough to make me suck in a breath when he raises a hand to scratch the top of his head. "What the fuck happened that has you flinching away from me? If your office isn't safe—"

"Nothing happened at work."

"But *something* happened," he says.

If a dog wants a bone, the best way to ease its focus is to give it a bone. I'll just make it a small bone. Snack sized.

"I stopped at my dad's house after work to change my clothes, and we had a disagreement. It rattled me, that's all. I'd forgotten how he can get sometimes."

"How does he get, Isabel?" Each word comes out of Cam's mouth with careful intent. His jaw ticks and his lips form a hard line, as if he's holding back, waiting for me to fill in the blank when he already knows the answer.

Of course, he knows. Everyone in town probably knows. And if anyone would, it's Cam. Tony must have told him some of the details over the years.

"He was drunk. Not good-times Edward Burns who buys rounds for everyone in the bar, drunk. Spent the day drinking alone and feeling sorry for himself, Edward Burns. I tried to quietly go in and out, to just avoid him, but he was rooting through the kitchen cupboards in search of a bottle that wasn't empty, and had broken a bunch of dishes in the process."

"And you stopped to clean up his mess?"

"No. I stopped and told *him* to clean up his mess. Let's just say the suggestion didn't go over well, and leave it at that." I flinch again when Cam innocently reaches out to touch my arm.

"Yeah, I don't think I'm going to be able to leave it at that, Isabel. If he laid a finger on you, I need to know. Tony needs to know."

"He got pissed off and threw something at me. It didn't hit me. And I already called Tony. He knows everything."

Exhaling slowly, Cam pushes his fingers through his hair. One of his self-calming techniques. He's probably raging inside.

"I'm okay. Just rattled. And I'm not going back, so you don't have to worry about me. Tony's going to let me sleep on his couch until I can get an apartment."

"Have you spent more than five minutes sitting on Tony's couch? It might as well be a stone slab. It's like he went to the furniture store and asked for the model with the least cushioning."

"I could actually picture him doing that," I say with a short but much-needed laugh. "Just to dissuade people from lingering too long in his bachelor pad."

"Exactly. I have a better idea."

"If it involves you loaning me money for an apartment, the answer is no thank you."

"Not money. A room. With a bed."

"Where?" The tingling low in my belly tells me I already know what the answer will be. I just can't decide if I'm excited to hear it, or terrified.

"My house," he says. "You can move in tonight. I promise you'll be safe."

From Cam, or my dad the drunk, or things that go bump in the night? I can believe that. But living in a tiny two-bedroom house with Cam and all his endless hotness and sweetness... the real question is, will I be safe from myself?

CAM

"You don't have to go through with this," Isabel says as I unlock the door. "I won't hold your spontaneous goodwill offer against you. I appreciate how you've always looked out for me, but this is going to be a huge crimp in your lifestyle."

I resist putting my hand on her lower back as she enters the house. Anything that might upset her is a hard no. I gave her the thirty-second, three-sixty spin-around tour when she was here a couple of nights ago, but having her in my house now has a different feel.

"My lifestyle consists of eat, work, sleep, with some occasional TV watching. I don't party or have buddies over. I'm not dating or hooking up. The only thing that's going to change with you living here is that I'll have to throw on underwear before leaving my bedroom. That rule doesn't apply to you, though. You're welcome to walk around naked anytime."

The suggestion earns me a cute laugh and a playful swat. The sound is like music, and any physical contact is a good sign after her jumpiness in the shop earlier.

"That one's yours." I point at the closed door of the second bedroom. "It only has a single bed, but it's basically new, and only Shelby has slept on it. She stayed here for a while after our mom died. She's back in her own apartment now."

"I love how close your family is," Isabel says, moving around the small living room, gently touching things, smiling at the framed photos on the wall. Her attention lingers on the one of my parents. "I haven't seen your dad since I got back to town. How's he doing—aside from the broken hand, obviously. Is he still in the same house you grew up in?"

"He still owns the house, but hasn't lived in it since my mom passed. He was sleeping in the loft above the shop. Shelby and I let him think he was keeping it secret from us, because it was obviously something he needed for his grieving process."

"But he's not staying up there now, or I would have seen him. I guess you had to call him out after the hand injury? Evict him from the loft so he doesn't try to work before the doctor clears him?"

"Different timeline and reasons, but yeah, he's not bunking up there anymore."

"But he didn't go back to the house? I can see why it'd be hard for him to live in the place he shared with your mom. I remember how in love they were; those times Tony would bring me along when he was hanging out at your house, your parents were always hugging and kissing—like, *really* kissing—and laughing. Stuff my parents never did." The sigh she makes is part dreamy, but also a little sad. Then she blinks and clears her throat. "I'm surprised your dad isn't using your spare room, though I guess that's because you don't want him to know how many hours you're putting in at the shop while he's off, hmm?" she say, raising an eyebrow. "Is he staying with Shelby?"

A grunt pushes through my lips, and Isabel tilts her head in question. Might as well tell her, since she's bound to find out, regardless of the outcome. "He's staying with his brand-new girlfriend, who happens to be twenty years younger than him."

Isabel's pretty eyes nearly pop out of her head. "Holy shit. Did not see that plot twist coming."

"None of us did. Including my dad. Things between them happened fast. Really fucking fast."

"You don't sound on board with it," she says, circling back to stand in front of me. "You don't like the woman?"

"I don't know her. Hell, my dad barely knows her. But he swears he's in love with her." I drop onto one end of the couch, rubbing my hands over my five-o'clock shadow. I usually shower as soon as I get home, and I'm definitely in need of one. "Maybe he is in love with her. That's the part that worries me. I don't want to see him have his heart broken again. I don't know why he'd want to take that risk. Why anyone takes the risk."

"Your dad is the perfect example of why people risk their heart for a chance at love." Isabel settles on the cushion beside me, close enough that our legs touch, and just like that, she's the only thing in the room. "He knows how amazing loving somebody can be. Look at the life he had with your mom. I can't even imagine the pain of losing someone who means so much," she says, placing her hand on my leg while holding my gaze. "But I'm positive your dad would say the heartbreak of losing his wife was a worthy price to pay for all the happiness they shared. And I bet that's why he's willing to risk having his heart broken again."

"Is all that wisdom based on observation, or have you been in love?"

"Observation." A soft laugh spills from her smiling lips. "And many years of futile pining."

I want to tell her the pining wasn't futile, that it just took a long time for me to get on the same page. That if anyone is worth risking my heart for, it's her. But that's not what she wants now. At least, not from me.

"What about the shitty ex-boyfriend? You didn't love him before things ended?"

This time when she laughs, it's bitter. Humorless. "Not even for a minute. The guys I dated out west were cut from the same cloth as my dad. I think some part of me sought them out, hoping I could fix them, since I used to feel like we abandoned my dad. I know, I know, I should probably get therapy. I'm taking a total man break instead. A reset to clear out all the toxic-choices damage, because I still hope to have the big love someday."

"You'll have it."

"You sound pretty sure about that for a guy who'll only commit to things with four wheels and a Ford badge."

"Brat." I give her a wink while pushing up from the couch.

"You love it," she says, twisting around so she's propped up on the backrest, a big smile on her face as she watches me cross to the bathroom door.

So fucking pretty. Lighting the place up just by being here. Lighting my whole damn world up just by existing. Making me want all the things I've been too chickenshit to reach for.

"No more settling for fixer-uppers for you, Iz. You deserve a man who'll put in the work to make every page of your scrapbook a reality."

"Thank you," she says softly.

One hand on the bathroom doorknob, I nod, then tip my head toward my bedroom. "It's been a long day; I'm going to grab a shower and hit the sack. Help yourself to my stuff until we pick yours up tomorrow. T-shirts, shorts, sweats, whatever you're comfortable sleeping in. I'll leave a toothbrush on the counter in here for you, and you're welcome to anything and everything in the house. No need to ask, just take whatever you want."

"I'll do that."

I nod again, then put the closed bathroom door between us, so more stuff I never expected to say—especially to Isabel Burns—doesn't flow out of my mouth. Best thing I can do right now is wait for her to be ready, and hope I'm the man she wants when she is.

Chapter Seven

ISABEL

Lying in bed in his house, wearing one of his soft, Cam-scented t-shirts, knowing he's on the opposite side of the wall, freshly showered and probably minimally clothed... not good circumstances for making sensible decisions. I've made my share of wrong choices in my adult years. If I do this—go to Cam's bedroom and ask him to have sex with me—there'll be no going back. It could ruin our new friendship, and I really like what we're building. I really like *him*, I always have. I wanted him to be my first. My last. Some things aren't meant to be.

But he can be my present, even if it's just for one night.

With extra padding in certain places, I'm sure I'm not his ideal type, but he's attracted to me enough to have almost kissed me—twice. He cares about me on a level nobody else ever has, not even my mom or big brother. Cam has gone so far above and beyond for me, it's hard to believe we reconnected less than a week ago.

I know I can trust him. Not with my heart, but he doesn't want that. I understand why he's hesitant to let someone all the way in, and I wouldn't ask for that.

Slipping out of bed, I pad across the smooth hardwood and step into the living room. All the lights are off in the small house, as they were when I got ready for bed after Cam took his shower. If he left his room since I heard its door close half an hour ago, he did it in high-stealth mode. I don't think Cam's the sneaking-around type. Not in any way. He's been upfront about everything, even when it wasn't positive, since our first conversation. If he doesn't want to do this with me, he won't hesitate to say no.

After a deep breath, I knock on his bedroom door. A triple tap loud enough to get his attention if he's awake, but not obnoxious enough to disturb him if he's already asleep.

There's some creaking and shuffling noise, then a husky, "You can come in."

The scent of him surrounds me when I open the door and step inside. When I came in here earlier to borrow a t-shirt for sleeping, I took the liberty of pressing my face against his pillow. Younger me would have been so proud.

With him present in the room, all I have to do is inhale to get a fix of his masculine scent. "Were you sleeping?"

"No. Are you okay, do you need something?"

The bravery and conviction of a minute ago is gone, leaving me feeling like a bumbling fool, standing in the dark, with only her lifetime's worth of Cam fantasies to keep her company.

"Isabel?"

"Yes. I need…I need…"

He sits up in bed, his form becoming a silhouette in the moonlight streaming through his window. "Whatever it is can't be that bad."

"It's the opposite of bad. It's you. I need you."

"Well, you've got me. I'm right here. You want to talk?"

"Not really."

"All right, then what?"

Pulse pounding in my ears, I move to the bed and crawl on top. When my hand brushes his leg through the thin sheet, his muscles twitch and jerk.

"Careful where you're patting around." He chuckles as he says it, but it's deep and rough. "Whoa, that's far enough," he says, his fingers clamping around my wrist when I slide my hand up the length of his quadriceps, nearly reaching the top.

"What if I want to go all the way?" I shift to straddle his legs, my inner thighs bracketing just below his hip area where he's holding my left hand hostage.

"What're you doing right now, Iz?"

"Showing you what I need," I say, dragging my right hand over the sheet until I find his cock. It's hard and thick, and he groans when I grip it through the thin cotton. "Were you like this when I walked in, or are you hard because of me?"

"Both." Now it's my right hand he cuffs, halting my exploratory stroking. "What did you really come in here to ask for? Because I don't think this is it, no matter how much I'd like it to be."

"But it is. I need to feel wanted by a good man. Someone who likes me. Cares about me. A man who doesn't put me down to make themself feel bigger. I know you don't want a commitment, and I'm okay with that. I won't have expectations afterward, and it doesn't have to change anything between us. I just want to feel like I'm worth some effort. Like I'm important and valued. And you've given me that already, with the way you look at me, and listen, and help. And what you said to me in the living room, that I deserve a man who'll put in the work for me…"

"Was the truth," he says, his callused hands cupping my face.

I cup one of his hands and draw it downward, over my breast, then lower, between my legs. "Show me how it feels when a man puts in the work."

He groans while sliding two fingers along my pussy. "Fuck, Iz, you came in here without panties?"

"You gave me permission to walk around naked, remember?"

"Then this has to go," he says, pulling the t-shirt up and over my head. "And one more thing…"

I'm about to tell him there's nothing else to take off when a small lamp above the headboard comes on. Instinctively, I wrap my arms around myself, covering as much as I can.

His dark eyes lock with mine as he gently peels my hands away. "No hiding this sexy body. I turned the light on so I can see every inch of you."

"There are a lot of inches. Extras I need to get rid of."

"No, baby, you're perfect. Soft and curvy like a fucking goddess." Strong hands glide gently over my bare breasts, raising my nipples to hard peaks, and goose bumps over the rest of my body.

I pinch my eyes closed, shame flaring hot in my cheeks when his hands travel over the soft muffin top below my belly button. He can't find that part of me sexy. No man has, and especially not one as lean and muscular as Cam. But when his thumbs continue making soft sweeps there, I open my eyes and find him watching me, not a hint of disgust to be found.

"Beautiful," he says, firmly gripping one hip and growling as he kneads my cushiony flesh. "I'm going to lick you all over. Every sweet peak and valley." The hand on my belly slides down between my legs, the pads of his fingers finding my clit and rolling circles over it as if he's touched me a thousand times before.

The need to come coils tight, and my body takes the wheel, overriding my embarrassment, shamelessly rocking against his hand.

"That's a good girl. I've got you, beautiful. So fucking hot, riding my fingers. Show me how fucking sexy you are when you come."

This is *Cam*. Cam, talking dirty to me. Cam making me feel wanton and worshipped.

Head thrown back, I grind against his talented fingers, giving myself over to the sensation, to him. My breath catches, leaving in little high-pitched gasps as I come.

Rolling me onto my back, he holds himself above me, his gaze meeting mine. "If you could see yourself through my eyes, you wouldn't have a single doubt that you're beautiful and sexy. I'm honored you want me, Isabel. I'll give you everything you need." Then he dips lower, gently brushing his mouth across mine. A teasing almost-kiss that has me wrapping my arms and legs around him, desperate to bring him closer.

The first firm press of his lips is everything I imagined kissing Cam would be. Dominant yet soft. Warm. Delicious. I open for him, moaning as the tip of his tongue touches mine. Each second is deeper, hungrier.

Desperate for more of him, all of him, I slide my hands down his smooth back and grab his firm butt so I can pull him tighter on top of me. The thick, hard ridge of his cock presses against my clit, and I moan, my body tingling with readiness. Within seconds, I'm coming again, moaning into his mouth as I writhe beneath him.

"So fucking responsive," he says, pressing his forehead to mine.

"It's you, you're doing it."

"It's us, Iz."

I nod, biting my lip so I don't say too much, don't break this once-in-a-lifetime magic.

He pulls back enough to look into my eyes. "You okay?"

"More than okay. This is better than anything I imagined, Cam. Thank you."

Serious eyes stare down into mine as he strokes my face. "Don't thank me for doing something I've wanted since the first day you came back into my life. Everything that happens between us tonight is for me as much as it's for you."

"Then keep going," I say, swallowing the big ball of emotions down.

Desire flares in his eyes before he dips down and takes my bottom lip between his teeth, gently nipping before letting it slide free. The next kiss is lower, on the soft skin below my chin, an erogenous zone I didn't know I had—or one that only exists with Cam. Next comes my neck. He takes his time, savoring the column before trailing his tongue along the lines of my collarbones.

Every cell in my body is awake and buzzing by the time he reaches my breasts. "Oh god…" I arch my back as he takes one nipple into his hot, wet mouth and suckles it hard while firmly pinching the other between two fingers. Heat streaks from the point to between my legs. Desperate for pressure there, I try to close my legs, but there's a very hot man's body between them.

Cam's dark eyes flick up and meet mine. His mouth working its magic on my nipple, he catches my hand and draws it to my pussy, guiding our joined fingers over my sensitive clit until my eyes roll back in my head from coming.

"You don't have to do that," I say when he moves farther down my body to settle between my legs. "You've put in enough work."

"Eating your pussy isn't work. It's my pleasure."

I can count on one hand the number of times a guy has

gone down on me, and none of them stayed down there long enough to make me come. I never even got close.

The instant Cam's mouth is on my pussy, the difference between duty oral and eating pussy for pleasure is obvious. Cam's tongue and lips are everywhere. Licking, teasing, probing, sucking. *Slurping.* Sweet baby Jesus, the filthy, carnal sounds. Then his mouth seals over my clit, and he sucks it hard and fast, making stars explode behind my eyelids, growling as I clutch his head and come so hard I can barely breathe.

Four orgasms. With Cam. With the lights on.

I wait for the embarrassment to kick in. Nothing happens. Okay, *something* happens, but that something is Cam crawling up my body and kissing my mouth as hungrily as he did my pussy.

Between us, he notches the head of his cock at my entrance, moaning when I wiggle enough that the tip slips inside me. "Move like that again and I'm going to be balls-deep inside you, baby. Be sure this is what you want, because I'm a breath away from getting lost in you."

Beads of sweat dot his handsome face as he looks down at me, waiting, letting me decide.

I made this decision a long time ago. I just never thought it would happen. "I want this."

"I want you." One smooth thrust and he's balls-deep, groaning as he stills, buried deep inside me. "Iz, you feel so fucking good. Tell me what you like, baby."

"You," I whisper as he rolls his hips, filling me completely, perfectly. "Everything you do."

The way he looks at me then…it's more than sex. His lips seal over mine, his deep kisses matching the deep, rhythmic strokes of his cock. Making love. He's making love to me. And it's so perfect I could cry. This is the first time I always dreamed of. The man I've always wanted. The only one. His hand finds my hip and gently squeezes. As if he knows everything going through my head and heart, and he's telling me it's okay to feel them. To love him.

And I do. I'm always going to love Cam.

"Need to look at you, pretty girl." He shifts to his knees, holding my hips and my gaze while he thrusts into me, over and over, hard and deep. "You're so fucking beautiful."

I feel beautiful. Even with everything bouncing and jiggling.

My breath hitches as he presses his fingers to my clit. One touch and I'm ready. So close. "Harder." I breathe the word, moaning and panting as he delivers the perfect pressure.

He moans, fucking me faster. "Fuck—baby—squeezing me so fucking tight. Come for me, Iz. Come for me."

My orgasm unfurls like a spiral. Endless waves of white-hot, perfect pleasure.

Cam's long, rough moan fills the room, his cock throbbing deep inside me before he folds himself over me, wrapping me in his arms, his heavy breathing tickling my ear. He presses his lips to my head, nuzzling my hair. "You're perfect, Isabel. Don't ever forget that."

Not an *I love you*, but still words I'll cherish for the rest of my life.

"You don't have to cuddle me," I say, when he rolls to his side with me in his arms, tucked in front of him, then pulls the sheet over us. "I can go back to the other room."

"Or you can stay right here," his arms tighten around me, one hand spanning my belly and the other cupping a breast, "where I want you."

Exactly where I've always wanted to be.

Chapter Eight

CAM

Routine is the mother of alarms, but when I open my eyes Saturday morning, the clock on the bedside table tells me it's half past eight. I haven't slept this late since I was a kid. Even exhausted from work, I always wake up before five.

The reason for my extra sleep is still curled up in front of me. She must've turned during the night because she's facing me now. Still tucked under my arm, though. Her long auburn hair is fanned out behind her on the pillow, tempting me to reach up and run my fingers through it. But that'd wake her, and right now, I just want to take her in. Her soft face. The full lips I couldn't get enough of. So warm and sweet and sexy, like every other part of her.

How any man could look at her and not see the most beautiful woman in the world is a fucking mystery. Knowing that some of them treated her like she was anything less than perfect makes fury roll in my gut.

Maybe Tony has names of her exes, wants to join me for a trip out to Vancouver, where we can swap hitting the heavy bag for some assholes instead.

"You're staring," she says in a sleepy voice as her eyelids flutter open. "Was I snoring?"

"Rumbling louder than an old carburetor." I pull her against me when she groans. "I'm teasing. You were sleeping like an angel."

"Then why were you just lying there and staring?"

"Enjoying the view."

"Bedhead and pillowcase wrinkles do it for you, huh?"

"You got me." I wink as if it's nothing more than joking around. But it's the truth. I was already hooked, well on my way to being hers. Now I know I am.

"Close your eyes," she says, wiggling backward, out of my arms. "I know you saw all of me last night, but that was a whole make-Isabel-feel-good thing. I told you I wouldn't have expectations and I don't. That includes not expecting you to continue telling me I'm beautiful or sexy. Especially in the daylight."

My stomach balls into a knot. "I meant every word I said last night."

Her lips part, but before any words come out, there's a knock at the front door.

"Shit. Totally forgot I told my dad I'd meet him for breakfast this morning." I throw back my side of the sheet and push up from the bed, letting Isabel look her fill of my naked body, including my cock jutting out, tall and hard.

Pink floods her cheeks as she tries—and fails—not to stare.

Good. I take myself in hand, dragging my fist up from root to tip. "This isn't average morning wood. This is from waking up next to you, Isabel. Doesn't matter what time of day it is, or whether the lights are dim or it's full-on daylight, I think you're beautiful and sexy, and I want you."

"Cam, I…" Biting her lip, she wraps the sheet around her curvy body before getting out of bed. "I can stick to my promise of not having expectations, but I can't do casual with you. I still want the white picket fence someday, and I'll never find it if I keep playing in your yard."

Another knock echoes through the house, followed by my dad's, "You okay in there?" and the sound of my spare key turning the deadbolt.

Wide-eyed, Isabel hurries out of my room, her startled gasp overlapping a gruff cough from my dad.

"Apologies," he says, averting his eyes as Isabel continues on to the spare room, closing its door behind her. His attention snaps to me next. "Sorry, son. When you didn't show at the diner, didn't answer your phone or the door… well, you know."

"Yeah, I do." When you've lost someone you love to a freak accident, you have a tendency to worry about anything out of the ordinary. "Breakfast slipped my mind. Give me a minute to wash up and we can still go if you want."

Dad chuckles, nodding at the closed door Isabel's hiding behind. "Guess she got flustered and thought that was the bathroom? I can step outside while you get ready. Don't want to embarrass the young lady more than I already have."

"Actually, that's her room," I say, rubbing my hand over my hair. "Isabel's staying with me."

"Isabel?" Dad's eyebrows rise over wide eyes. "Tony's little sister?"

"The one and only."

Unlike a lot of parents, mine never judged, even when I gave them good reason to. So, when my dad says, "Do you think that's a good idea?" while pointing at Isabel's door, I know it's a big deal.

"She just moved back to town, doesn't have an apartment yet, and it's not safe for her to live at her dad's house. I have an empty room. Makes sense for her to use it."

"I wasn't talking about letting your best friend's little sister stay in your spare room, but you know that. Based on the expression on your face, you think I'm right about the activity I was referencing."

"It's not what you think." I blow out a breath. "It's not what she thinks, either."

"Well, if she's half as confused as I am, and you seem to be, it's probably best for you to skip our breakfast and go talk to her."

The spare room door opens and Isabel steps out, chin held high, dressed in her clothes from yesterday. "I'm going to swing by dad's and pick up a few things if the coast is clear. I'll see you later."

"I'll move the car so you can get yours out of Cam's garage," Dad says, following her out.

I bite my tongue, but I know what's coming. And it does. The moment my dad steps inside the house again.

"Isabel's driving the Bronco." A big old smile stretches across his face. "How long have you been in love with her, and when do you plan to tell her with words?"

"Today. But not with words. With a fence. Feel like hitting the building center with me?"

"Let's go," Dad says, clapping me on the shoulder. "But if I can give you a word of advice—say the words. As soon as you can, and as often as you can."

CAM

It's mid-afternoon by the time Isabel turns into the driveway. The garage door is open, but she doesn't pull in. She stops immediately, parking on the asphalt and hopping out of the Bronco. Standing in front of it, she stares at the front yard where I set up short, white plastic garden fencing around the perimeter.

"Is this a joke?" she asks when I join her. Her eyebrows are drawn together and her lips are curved in a direction that says she doesn't think it's funny.

"No, baby. It's a promise." Wrapping my arms around her, I pull her tight against me. "Best I could do with limited time, but the lumber for a real fence is in the garage."

She blinks up at me, lips parted, her eyes full of unspoken questions. Hopes and dreams and so much emotion.

"I want to build the white picket fence with you. I want it to be our yard, to play in together for the rest of our lives. Just the two of us, or if you still want those kids from your scrapbook, I would be fucking honored to be their father.

I'm still scared shitless of losing you one day, but the thought of a life without you being part of every minute and every memory because I didn't take the risk... that's a hell of a lot scarier." Time to take my dad's advice. "I love you, Isabel. I am head-over-heels in love with you."

"Cam," she whispers, tears rolling down her cheeks. "I'm scared."

"I'll never hurt you, Iz. I promise. I know you probably think this is too fast, but I know what I want. I want you. I want this, us. Come home to me, baby. Every day, for the rest of your life."

"I love you," she says, throwing her arms around my neck and burrowing against my chest. "You've always been my home."

"I have something else for you. Well, for us, since I want us to use it together."

She pulls back and smiles up at me, her eyebrows wiggling, then shooting up her forehead when I release her to jog back to the garage. "Am I supposed to follow you? Is it *another* old truck? Where the *Ford* are we going to put them all?"

I shake my head while walking toward her, grinning like a kid at Christmas. Only, I'm happier than that. Because of her. "A little smaller than a truck, but with the space to be as big as we can dream," I say, handing her the scrapbook. Blank inside, except for one picture of us from when we were kids.

"Oh, Cam..." Fresh tears well in her eyes when she opens it. Smiling, she runs her fingertips over the photo. "I remember this day."

"I thought it was a good beginning."

"It's perfect," she says, pulling my head down for a kiss.

And it is. Just like the rest of our story will be.

Epilogue

Six weeks later

CAM

I nearly drop the tray of sirloin patties, chicken breasts, and vegan burgers when I step out the back door onto the patio. "Fucking gorgeous."

Isabel looks over her shoulder toward me, a big smile on her face. "High praise for string lights, cutesy Ford-themed decorations, and a handmade banner, but I'll take it."

"Your setup out here looks great and I appreciate all the work you did planning this dinner for my dad, but the 'gorgeous' was for you."

She must've changed while I was in the kitchen prepping the barbecue stuff because the body-hugging teal dress she's wearing is new. Not just a change from the cute little ass-revealing denim shorts and cutoff t-shirt she had on while decorating the backyard. *New,* new. As in, I haven't seen her wear it in the seven weeks since she got back to town. Something that shows off her irresistible curves like this? I would definitely remember.

"I haven't seen you in this dress before, and it makes me want to see you out of it."

"Well, good," she says, sliding her arms around my waist after I set the tray of cookables on a side table near the barbecue. "That's exactly the effect I wanted it to have."

"It's the effect you always have on me, no matter what you're wearing." I don't care that my family is due to arrive any minute, I slide my hands over Isabel's body, molding my roughened palms to the sides of her breasts, then her waist, the full hips I love to grab while we're fucking, and last but certainly not least, her juicy round ass.

After a bit of manual exploration, I nuzzle the spot in front of her ear that always makes her shiver. "I don't feel any panties under this slippery material. Did you forget them?"

Her soft hair brushing my skin when she shakes her head sends a rush of awareness to my cock. "I wanted to tease you. Is it working?"

I capture one of her hands and drag it to the front of my jeans. "You tell me," I say, dragging her hand up and down the hard bulge beneath my fly. "Feel what you do to me, Iz. Six weeks of having you every single day and I still want more."

The stiffening in her posture is slight, but noticeable to me. There's not much I don't register where Isabel is concerned. I've been addicted to her since the day she walked back into my life. She's my everything.

Shifting from borderline groping her to gently stroking her back, I lift her chin with my other hand until our eyes meet. "I felt you tense up. Something wrong?"

"I'm fine." The small smile she gives doesn't cover the quiver in her bottom lip or the glassiness in her pretty eyes. "We should get the salads out of the fridge."

"We won't need salads or anything else if I tell everyone to turn around and go home, which is what I'll do if you're upset about something. And don't tell me you're not, because I felt it the moment you switched from light and happy to whatever you are now."

Dark eyelashes flutter against the tops of her cheeks as she averts her gaze. "Everything is so perfect and you've made all my dreams come true. Then sometimes I get this tight, panicky feeling, like, one of the times you look at me, you're going to snap out of it."

That she could think that, on any level, for even a fraction of a moment, sets my stomach churning.

My family is notorious for showing up at inopportune times, and this is no exception. I hear the telltale rumble of Dad's '67 Mustang out front. "Shit."

"I'm fine," Isabel says again. "I just had a blip of insecurity. Please don't let it ruin this get-together with your family."

"Nothing is going to be ruined tonight." Taking her hand, I lead her from the patio toward the garage, waving at my dad and Dove as they get out of the Mustang. "Help yourselves to a drink. Isabel and I will be there in a few minutes."

"Take your time," Dad calls, returning the wave. Even he doesn't know what I had planned for Isabel, and I tell him damn near everything.

"Cam, this isn't necessary. I don't need to talk about my crazy feelings." Isabel might as well give her protest to a brick wall.

When I make up my mind to do something, especially where she's concerned, there's no going back. I hadn't planned to do *this* until Christmas. But I've also been carrying the means to do it around in my pocket, just in case the perfect moment presented itself sooner. Maybe now isn't picture-perfect, but it's right.

At the man door of the garage, I reach into my pocket and come out with two items, though all Isabel sees are my keys. I extend my arm toward the lock and *accidentally* drop the keys on the ground.

Instead of leaning over or crouching to retrieve them, I drop to one knee in front of her. Hold up the ring. Stare up into the wide-open eyes of the woman I love. "I had planned to do this at Christmas, in front of our first tree, with all the twinkling lights and decorations we pick out together. I even made a scrapbook page for it. But I was only waiting because I wanted to make it a special memory. And the real truth is that every memory we make is special. You're all I think about. The only woman I've been in love with, the only one I will ever want. Forever, Isabel. Make me the happiest man alive and wear my ring. Grant me the absolute privilege of being your husband."

"Oh, Cam," she whispers.

"That's not a yes, baby. Going to need to hear a yes."

"Yes, yes, yes!" Her face lights up and she squeals while offering me her left hand, its fingers waggling excitedly. "I've been waiting for this since the third grade."

Grinning up at her, I slide the band onto her finger, then stand and pull her into my arms. "Thank you for waiting for me," I say, dipping down to kiss her sweet, warm lips.

But we don't get long to be lost in each other. We have an audience on the patio now—Dad and Dove, Shelby and Brody, the new hire—and they're making themselves known with applause and whistling.

"I love you," she says, resting her head against my chest.

I press my lips to her soft hair. "And I love you."

"You know I'm going to need to see that scrapbook page, right?"

A laugh as natural as breathing rocks both of us as I hold her. The kind of laugh she always inspires. "It's yours, baby. It's all yours." And she's all mine.

THANK you for reading *Driver's Seat*! I hope you enjoyed this quick, sweet, blue-collar-hero romance.

Shifting Gears is Cam's dad's book! If you love a sexy silver fox who's good with his hands, you'll fall in love with Granger Smith.

Shifting Gears is available now in ebook and paperback.

JOIN KARLA'S mailing list for up-to-date news about new releases, sales, freebies, and more!

https://www.karladoyle.com/newsletter/

SHIFTING GEARS

UNDER THE HOOD SERIES – BOOK 1

Thirty years of elbow grease and commitment have made Under the Hood one of the busiest garages in town. I live and breathe work since my wife died. My kids encourage me to move on, meet someone new, but they don't know what I know—soulmates happen once in a lifetime, if you're lucky.

That doesn't mean my eyes don't work, and I can't take mine off my newest customer. The friendly, flirty brunette wants me to do a lot more than fix her car, and God help me, I'm tempted. I'm drawn to her in ways I never expected to experience again.

Dove is beautiful and smart, she's also twenty years younger than me. Her touch is like jumper cables to my heart, but can she repair all the broken parts of me?

CHAPTER ONE

GRANGER

"Good morning," my daughter, Shelby calls from the doorway separating the front office from the automotive bays. "We don't open for twenty minutes and you've already moved all the cars out of the shop. How early do I have to wake up to beat you here in the morning?"

I know she's joking. I also know she wouldn't like hearing the truth—she couldn't beat me to the shop, because I've been here since yesterday. And the day before that, and the day before that. I won't tell her the truth but I won't lie to her either. I'll detour. That'll do the trick.

"I've been the first person here every day since I opened the place. Don't see that routine changing anytime soon, so you might as well enjoy the extra half hour of sleep." I toss the rag I've been using to wipe my bench, and head toward my daughter. "How's the schedule look this morning? Much coming in at eight o'clock?"

"An oil change with a front-end check. An alignment after getting new tires. The alignment is here all day, I said we'd squeeze it in when we had an opening. Bill Martin is dropping off his car for front and back brakes."

"Both? I thought we were just doing the front brakes this morning. Back brakes with his winter tire changeover."

Shelby moves to the counter to read the schedule, then faces me again, this time with narrowed eyes. "You're right, it is just front brakes today. You checked before you asked me, didn't you?"

Can't detour around this one. Best option is to stretch the truth. "I glanced as I walked by and Bill's name jumped out at me, so I took a look at the note by his name."

"I see." That's Shelby code for *I don't believe you but I'll drop the subject.* She picked that one up from her mother.

Sometimes she reminds me so much of Eline, it takes everything in me not to turn away. Eighteen months has dulled the ache, but the pain's still there, lingering below the surface, ready to grab hold and drag me down again.

Shelby's hand on my arm brings me back to the present. "You totally zoned out there. Did you skip breakfast again?"

"You caught me," I say, taking advantage of the excuse. I pull out my phone and tap the screen until Cam's name appears. "I'll text your brother to pick up donuts and coffee."

"Text him whatever you want, Dad, but you're not touching donuts until you eat some fruit and a yogurt."

"Can't eat what you don't have."

"Good thing you have both. There's a bunch of bananas on the breakroom table and yogurt is in the fridge."

"That's your food." Even as I say it, I have a feeling I won't win this one. Just like I never could with her mother.

"The food is *ours.* I expensed it to the shop, so you have no excuse to turn it down or skip meals."

"Think you're pretty smart, don't you?"

"Yes. Now go eat." She waves me away with one hand while reaching for the ringing phone with the other.

"Under the Hood, this is Shelby. How can I help you today?"

Eline taught her to answer the phone that way. One hell of a mouthful in my opinion, but customers seem to like it. Eline always had a way with people. Made them comfortable and at ease, whether she was booking an appointment or quoting thousands of dollars' worth of work. Shelby hasn't mastered the technical stuff yet, but she has the same knack for making people feel relaxed.

I'm lucky to have her here. I should tell her that more often, instead of micro-managing her, the way I did with the schedule. If I *do* continue checking her work, I need to keep my damn mouth shut. It won't matter if she makes a mistake here or there. The business can afford to cover a few extra parts or unbilled labor hours. Under the Hood has been profitable since I started it. We'll be fine, even if business slows down a bit. Hell, even if it slows down a lot.

In the breakroom, I grab a strawberry yogurt from the fridge and take a seat at the new table. Some build-it-yourself thing Shelby and Cam put together, after donating the one I had before. I pull a spoon from the covered, plastic storage container that replaced the old coffee can of cutlery. The walls surrounding me are now a bluish color, instead of the original creamy-yellow. Shiny-new, gray filing cabinets have taken over for the beaten-up brown ones I bought over two decades ago. All Shelby's doing, in the name of updating the place.

We don't talk about the *other* reason for Shelby's modifications.

There are still times I walk into a room and expect to see my wife. Less frequently since Shelby's wall-to-wall changes. Being at the shop is easier now. Good thing, since I have nowhere else to go. The house is…not for me. Not anymore. It takes everything in me to spend time there without Eline. I rarely try.

Shelby doesn't know that, though. Neither does Cam. And that's the way it's going to stay.

"There's a no-start getting towed in," Shelby says, hanging up the phone. "New customer. Should be here by eight, but I told her she'll have to leave it because we won't get to it immediately."

"Sounds good." I scrape the last spoonful of yogurt, rinse the spoon in the sink, and throw the empty container in the recycling box on my way out.

"Hold on there." Shelby issues a clothesline as I cut through the office, heading for the shop. "I didn't see you eat any fruit."

"No, you didn't."

"Dad."

"I'll have some later," I say. "When I stop for a break."

"You never take a break."

"Maybe I will today."

"I'm not ten years old anymore. I know that 'maybe' is just another word for 'no.'"

I shoot her a wink. "We'll see."

"Also a 'no' in disguise." She withdraws her outstretched arm and shakes her head while resuming work at the computer. "You should try listening to me sometimes."

"I do listen. Sometimes."

Her exaggerated grumble puts a smile on my face. Maybe I'll take a break this morning, to show her I do listen. Maybe.

Out in the shop, I tidy the top of my workbench. Wipe yesterday's greasy handprints from the cordless phone, then give the laptop's keyboard a swipe. A couple of clicks and I could check the parts orders. Make sure we're getting everything we need for this morning's jobs, because, although Shelby didn't mention it, Bill needs his car back by eleven o'clock. He always needs it done by eleven.

Experience has taught me that parts for Bill's BMW are rarely in stock at any of the local suppliers. If Shelby didn't order the pads and rotors before closing yesterday, we'll have to scramble to get parts here on time. I hate scrambling.

If I check the order history and don't see an invoice for the parts, I can make some calls, get stuff here by ten-thirty. Cam would have to step away from his bay and help when the parts arrive, but together, we could bang the job off in time. The downside to that plan—Shelby would know I've checked her work. *Again.*

"Shit." I toss the rag on the keyboard. "Damned if I do, and damned if I don't."

"Maybe this'll help," Cam says, setting a large coffee next to my laptop. "If not, this might." A small paper bag joins the takeout cup. "Don't let Shelby see that. She already warned me not to share my 'shit food' with you."

"So, she's okay with *you* eating donuts, but not me."

"She knows it's pointless to harass me." Cam bites into his donut. Two more bites and the donut's gone. "And she worries about you. Thinks it's her job to take care of you, until you find somebody else to do the job." He uses the back of his hand to clear the powdered sugar dusting his upper lip. "Anything to report on that front?"

"No, and that's the way it's going to stay." The sooner my kids accept my decision to be alone, the happier we'll all be.

No comment from Cam, just a shrug as he walks away. Temporary silence, no doubt. My son never argues with me. The subject will be back though, probably sooner than later. Cam might not argue, but he isn't one to take "no" for an answer if he thinks "yes" is a better choice. Damn set in his ways, that one.

Both my kids are.

I turn, using my body to shield the bag from view, then cough to cover the crinkle of paper as I remove the donut. Jelly-filled, my favorite. Nice and fresh, too.

"Dad."

Ah, hell. Busted. I set the donut on my torque wrench, and turn toward the sound of Shelby's approaching footsteps. "The filling counts as fruit."

"What?" Her eyes narrow at first, then her gaze shifts to the donut. "Ugh. You're impossible."

"Good you've finally accepted that."

"Acknowledging a thing isn't the same as accepting it." She steps forward, picks up the donut and bites off half. Jelly streaks her lips. She chews a few times, swallows, then shoves the remainder of the pastry into her mouth.

"Nicely done," Cam says, reaching past me to grab the ringing phone, since Shelby's stuffed chipmunk cheeks prevent her from answering. "Under the Hood." No longwinded introduction from him. Just the basics.

Shelby nods at him, finishes chewing and swallows, shaking her head in the process. "You have to stop eating that crap, Dad."

"I don't care if I get fat."

"I'm not worried about your weight. I'm worried about your heart."

No amount of healthy eating will change the status of my heart. It was damaged beyond repair the day Eline took her last breath. "You worry too much. Stop thinking about my life and focus on doing something fun for a change."

"Yeah, Shelb," Cam says, replacing the phone on the cradle. "Focus on doing *somebody* fun for a change."

She swipes at her brother, missing, as she always does. "Fun guys always turn out to be temporary and undependable. I want somebody I can count on."

Exactly what a father wants to hear. Though, letting loose now and then wouldn't hurt, either. Shelby's too young to be sitting home, eating responsibly and getting a good night's sleep, seven days a week.

I nod at the clipboards Shelby's tucked under her arm. "What've you got?"

She waves the first work order in Cam's direction. "Oil change with a front-end check. Clunking noise when they turn right. They're sitting up front." She waits for Cam to take the clipboard, then hands the second one to me. "You get Bill's BMW. I ordered the parts yesterday afternoon. I just checked, they should be here within ten minutes."

"Great." Shame on me for not trusting her to stay on top of the jobs. Lesson learned. "I'll bring it in and start tearing it apart."

She nods. "I'm giving Bill a lift to work. I'll be right back."

"Sounds good. We'll get the phones and keep an eye on the front."

She leaves without another word, all hustle and focus. A minute later, the front door bell chirps, signaling her exit.

I take a swig of coffee, then another for good measure. Metal snaps against wood as I pull the BMW keys from beneath the clip. I toss the clipboard on my toolbox and head toward the bay door, grabbing a seat protector and disposable floor mat along the way. Before I've taken two strides across the gravel, a red tow truck pulls into the lot with a compact sedan on board.

"Morning." I nod at Frank as he hops out from the driver's side of the carrier truck. "Is this the no-start?"

"Yep." He nods toward the truck, as the passenger door opens. "She's new in town, so I recommended you."

"Thanks." I lean in while clapping him on the shoulder. "Why didn't you also recommend she send her car, but stay home?"

He laughs. "I did. She wasn't interested." His eyes twinkle as a woman exits the cab of his truck. "You might be glad about that, after you meet her. A real looker. And no wedding ring."

Shit. As if Cam and Shelby hounding me isn't bad enough. I want to find wherever it's written that a widower has to find a new woman, and set that damn book on fire.

One look at the sedan's owner tells me I can forget about the matches and gasoline. Oh, she's a looker, all right. Just because I don't want to be with another woman, doesn't mean I don't appreciate them. I'd have to be blind not to notice this one. Pretty face, friendly smile, nice figure. But she's younger. Cam's age, not mine.

Since Shelby's not here, maybe Cam should come out and do the talking. He's never had trouble meeting women, but he hasn't shown any serious interest in one since his mother passed. I'd bet every last tool I own that those things are directly related. Fair's fair. If my son can butt into my personal life, I can do the same.

"Dashboard lit up like a Christmas tree, then the car died. Wouldn't boost for me," Frank says, as the attractive brunette walks toward us.

"Got it."

He takes my comment for the dismissal it is, tipping his hat at the woman as he heads to his truck.

"Give me a sec to send someone out," I tell the customer standing in front of me. "Cam can take your information and give you a hand."

"Wait." She halts my getaway by reaching for my arm. "Are you Granger?"

I look down at her delicate fingers, curled over my bare forearm. Aside from my daughter's hugs, it's the first female contact I've had since my wife died. And it's…

Gone. "Sorry," she says, obviously mistaking my expression for something negative, and yanking her hand away.

"No need to be." The smile I give might as well be plastic. Better that than gawking at her like a creepy, old fart who thinks a random, generic touch is some sort of subtle come-on. "And, yes, I'm Granger."

"Great." She extends her hand again, this time offering it for me shake.

Which I do, because I'm polite and professional. Not because I want to feel her warm, soft fingers on my skin again.

"Dove Ellis. I'm new to the area."

"Dove? That's a pretty name."

"Thanks." She takes the compliment in stride, though the sparkle in her eyes tells me there's more commentary going on internally.

And, damn, if I don't want to hear every word of it.

"I moved from Toronto a couple weeks ago. Sid Morton is my neighbor. He told me you're the only person who should be looking under my hood." A throaty little laugh leaves her rosy-pink lips. "And, yes, those were his exact words."

"Sounds like something he'd say, and then think he's the funniest guy around for saying it." It appears I have another nosy parker in my life, only this one's name is Sid.

"He does like to crack a lot of jokes."

I'm nodding along, staring at her mouth as it curves into a smile. I can't stop, even though I know I look like an idiot.

"So…" she says, laughing lightly while glancing at our joined hands.

I release the hand I've been shaking continuously for at least twenty seconds. "Sorry about that. My mind's always on half a dozen things when we first open."

"Oh, of course." She crosses her arms over her chest, an action that pushes her breasts upward, giving me yet another thing to avoid ogling.

I need to get Cam out here. Retreat to the safe depths of the shop, before I do something more foolish than I already have. Since Cam just took off for a test drive of his eight o'clock appointment, looks like I'm on the hook to talk to Dove. Something I should have no problem doing. I've talked to thousands of people in my thirty years running the shop.

"The tow truck driver filled me in about your car," I say, forcing my eyes north of the row of tiny buttons that ends at the valley of Dove's cleavage.

She nods. "He said it's probably the alternator."

"Sounds like it, but we'll test everything once we have an opportunity to bring it into the garage. We're booked solid this morning, so that might not happen until after lunch. I hope my daughter told you that when you called."

"She did. I knew I'd have to leave my car for the day, at least. That's no problem, I work from home."

I don't ask why she bothered to come down with the tow truck. Lots of people can't let their car go, they worry it'll end up at the wrong shop. I'm sure that's all it is with this woman.

Dove uncrosses her arms, slides her fingertips into the pockets of some very tight jeans, and shifts her weight to one leg. The position accentuates the curve of her left hip. It's jutted out like a handle, tempting me to grab it.

What the hell is with me this morning? I haven't had thoughts like this since Eline died. And I've certainly never had them about any woman other than the one love of my life. My body's telling me it's overdue for release, that's all. I don't need a woman for that. Just a few extra minutes in the shower.

I nod and gesture toward the office door with the sweep of an arm. "I'll grab your phone number inside. Shelby will call you with an estimate before we do any work. She's out dropping someone off, but she can give you a lift home when she gets back."

"Sounds good, thank you." She smiles while brushing past me, close enough that her arm grazes mine.

Opening the door creates a vacuum that circulates whatever perfume she's wearing. The light, floral scent fills my nose, and like a damn fool, I inhale deeply—an action that doesn't go unnoticed.

She pauses in the small vestibule, bringing us into close proximity. Very close. "I can wait outside if my perfume bothers you."

The phone is ringing in the office. I should be hustling in there to pick it up, but I'm frozen, nearly chest-to-chest with this beautiful woman I just got caught smelling. It's not the embarrassment that's holding me in place, it's her. The hazel eyes looking straight into mine, the pulse beating in her neck, the rise and fall of her breasts. And her scent… God help me, I can't get enough of it.

"It's fine. You're—good." There's a huskiness to my voice I couldn't mask if I tried, so I leave it at that.

"Okay," she says. But she doesn't just turn and go into the office. She pulls her bottom lip into her mouth, releasing it slowly as she smiles. She lifts her hand and places it on my arm again, sending a streak of electricity racing to parts of my body I thought were dead. "I'm glad my neighbor sent me down here to meet you."

"So am I." The words are out of my mouth before my brain has a chance to kick in. Shit. Time to get a hold on myself, shift back to mechanic mode, where I belong. I edge backward, forcing her hand to fall away. "We're always happy to help our customers. I'm sure we'll have you back on the road soon."

Her smile falters, then she turns and walks into the office ahead of me, not saying another word.

Which is what I wanted. So, why the hell does it feel like I just made a huge mistake?

~

Shifting Gears is available now in ebook & paperback. Get your copy today!

Also by Karla Doyle

Paranormal Romances:

Now You See Me (Screaming Woods)

Snake Believe (Screaming Woods)

Once Upon A Beast (Hemlock Woods)

The Beast Within (Hemlock Woods)

Mated to the Minotaur (Fate's Falls)

The Grumpy Demon's Sunshine (Fate's Falls)

A Reaper is Forever (Fate's Falls)

Falling for the Yeti (Fate's Falls)

Contemporary Romances:

Wedded Miss

Dad Bod Wingman (Hope Harbor)

Heart Beats (Hope Harbor)

Last Call Casanova (Hope Harbor)

Fleshing It Out (Hope Harbor)

The Deal With Love (Hope Harbor)

Doggy Style (Hope Harbor)

Resorting to Love (linked to Hope Harbor)

White Lie Christmas (linked to Hope Harbor)

King of Her Dreams (Hope Harbor)

Heart of Texas (linked to Hope Harbor)

Her Pipe Dream (Hope Harbor)

12 Days (Hope Harbor)

Puck That

Shifting Gears (Under the Hood)

Driver's Seat (Under the Hood)

Gingerbread Man (Man of the Month: Candy Cane Key)

Just in Queso (Man of the Month: Magnolia Point)

Unexpected Addition

Dating the Doubter

Gift Wrapped

Cup of Sugar (Close to Home #1)

Icing on the Cake (Close to Home #2)

Sweet as Candy (Close to Home #3)

Body of Work (Very Personal Training #1)

Worth the Wait (Very Personal Training #2)

Game Plan

More Than Words

Crossing the Line

Visit Karla's website for the most up-to-date list.

http://www.karladoyle.com

See Karla's books sorted by tropes and themes!

https://www.karladoyle.com/books/by-tropes/

About the Author

A small-town girl with some big-city experience, Karla resides in Southwestern Ontario with her husband and two amazing, young-adult kids. She studied fashion design in college and spent 20+ years working in that industry before succumbing to the writing muse. When she's not writing the sexy stories that swirl around in her head, you can find her spending time with family, hanging out with book-loving friends on Facebook, or cuddled up with a book and her adorable pets.

Karla loves hearing from readers! Connect with her online, or send her an email: karla@karladoyle.com.

Join Karla's mailing list to stay up to date on all her news.